THE CHESTNUT SOLDIER

The Magician Trilogy
Book Three

JENNY NIMMO

SCHOLASTIC INC.
New York Toronto London Auckland Sydney
Mexico City New Delhi Hong Kong Buenos Aires

For Myfanwy

This book was originally published in hardcover in the United States by Orchard Books in April 2007.

ISBN-13: 978-0-545-07127-7
ISBN-10: 0-545-07127-5

Copyright © 1989 by Jenny Nimmo.

First published in 1989 in Great Britain by Methuen Children's Books Ltd. All rights reserved. Published by Scholastic Inc. SCHOLASTIC and associated logos are trademarks and/or registered trademarks of Scholastic Inc. ORCHARD BOOKS and design are registered trademarks of Watts Publishing Group, Ltd., used under license.

12 11 10 9 8 7 6 5 4 3 2 1   9 10 11 12 13 14/0

Printed in the U.S.A.   40

First Scholastic paperback edition, January 2009

Text type set in Garamond 3
Display type set in Dalliance Roman
Book design by Marijka Kostiw

CONTENTS

Prologue

IT IS FOUR YEARS SINCE GWYN GRIFFITHS DISCOVERED HE WAS
a magician. In Book One, *The Snow Spider*, Gwyn's mystic grandmother gives him five unusual gifts: a Celtic brooch, a piece of
seaweed, a tin whistle, a small wooden horse, and a scarf that
belonged to Gwyn's sister, Bethan. Bethan disappeared one
stormy night on the mountain behind the Griffiths's farmhouse,
and Gwyn has always longed to find her again.

On his grandmother's instructions, Gwyn throws four of his
gifts to the wind and a magical silver spider appears. Gwyn
calls her Arianwen, meaning white-silver. She helps Gwyn
bring his sister back from the Otherworld, a place of snow and
ice, inhabited by pale children with white hair. But Bethan is
not allowed much time with her family. Soon she has to return
to her icy planet, on a silver ship that comes out of the sky.

Two years later, in Book Two, *Emlyn's Moon*, Gwyn meets his
long-lost cousin, Emlyn, the son of a famous painter. At first
the two boys are enemies, but they are brought together by Nia
Lloyd, a shy girl who can't believe she will ever achieve anything important.

The pale children from the Otherworld reappear. This time they want to take Emlyn away with them, and as Gwyn and Nia try to save him, Nia begins to understand her true talent.

There is one gift that Gwyn's grandmother tells him he must never use: the small carving of a broken horse. It lies, hidden, in Gwyn's room, guarded by Arianwen, the silver snow spider. But the evil spirit within the horse is merely biding its time, waiting for the day when someone will set it free.

CHAPTER ONE

An Unexpected Caller

THE PRINCE DID NOT COME ENTIRELY UNANNOUNCED! THERE were messages. They slipped through the air and invaded Gwyn's fingers; his joints ached, things fell out of his grasp, and he knew something was on its way.

They had nearly finished the barn; it only needed a few extra nails on the roof to secure it against the wild winds that were bound to come, and planks to fit for the lambing pens. That was Gwyn's task. He had never been much of a carpenter and today he was proving to be a disaster. But he could not pretend that cold or damp was causing his clumsiness. A huge September sun glared across the mountains, burning the breeze. The air was stifling!

Gwyn hated hammering on such a day. Sounds seemed to sweep unimpeded into every secret place, and with his father on the roof banging away at corrugated iron, the clamor was deafening.

"Aww!" Gwyn dropped his hammer into a bucket of nails and thrust his fist against his mouth.

"What've you done, boy?" Ivor Griffiths called from his perch.

"Hammered my thumb, didn't I?"

"You need glasses!"

"Take after you then, don't I?" It was a family joke, Ivor's glasses. They were always streaked with mud or lost. Gwyn could see them now, balanced on a pile of planks.

"Is it bad?" his father asked.

"Mmm-hmm!" Pain began to get the better of Gwyn; the numbing ache was aggravated by a bruised and bleeding thumbnail.

"Better go and see Mom," his father suggested. "You're no use injured, are you?"

"No, Dad!" Gwyn slid a chisel into his pocket, wondering why he felt compelled to do this. Perhaps something at home needed his attention. He didn't know, then, what it would be.

He stuck his thumb in his mouth and jogged down the mountain track toward the farmhouse. In spite of the urgency, he could not resist a look back at the barn. It would be a grand shelter for the ewes, something to be proud of, for they'd done it all themselves: he and his dad, his cousin Emlyn, and Uncle Idris. It was a family affair.

"Idiot!" Gwyn told himself. "There's nothing going on here." It was such a bright and beautiful day. He could see it all from his high field, and all was well. Nothing threatened from the valley, where trees glowed with early autumn color. There were no phantoms hiding in the mountains that stretched calm and splendid under an empty sky. But the warning in his hands could not be ignored.

He was tired of magic, of intuition and the unnatural power

that rippled through him sometimes. Once, he'd been tall for his age. But in four years he'd hardly grown. Now information slipped in and out of his mind too swiftly for him to make sense of it. In class he dreamed, wondered about the distance between stars instead of trees, drew crescents where he should have made straight lines, forgot his English, and wrote Welsh poetry that no one understood.

Perhaps soon, he thought, *when I am thirteen, the wizard in me will fade away and I will grow and be like an average boy.* To be average was Gwyn's greatest wish.

Bending his head over his injured thumb, Gwyn began to run, really hard this time, so that the stitch in his side would distract him from the painful little hints of bad tidings.

❊ ❊ ❊

His mother was in the kitchen, baking for the school fair. Her face glowed pink, with triumph or the unnatural temperature, Gwyn couldn't guess which. The long table was mounded with extravagantly decorated cakes, and the stove was still roaring. Mrs. Griffiths had a reputation to maintain. Her cooking won prizes. Two sticky flypapers hung above the table, diverting insects from chocolate sponge cakes, iced doughnuts, cakes layered with jam, and waves of fruitcake. The papers buzzed with dead and dying creatures.

"Oh! It's hot in here, Mom!" Gwyn exclaimed. "How can you stand it?"

"I don't have a choice, do I?" Mrs. Griffiths mopped her flushed cheeks with a damp tissue. "Your dad's not shoveled the manure from the yard, and if I open the window, there'll be such a stench and swarms of flies all through the house. I don't know how the wasps get in, the sly things!"

"Dad's still working on the barn. He's nearly done. It's going to be just great, Mom!"

"I know! I know! What've you done to yourself?" She eyed Gwyn's bloody thumb.

"Hammered my fingernail." Gwyn grinned sheepishly.

"You're not going to tell me it was the cold that made you clumsy?"

"Naw! It was the sun, made my eyes water." It was a pretty lame excuse since he'd been inside the barn, but it would have to do. He gave up all attempt at bravery and grimaced. "It hurts, Mom!"

"Come on then, let's run cold water on it!" His mother took his hand.

The water was icy. It calmed the pain in his thumb, but now his fingers tingled unbearably. Something needed to be done, but what? "That's enough! I'm OK!" He pulled his hand away.

"It's still bleeding, Gwyn. I'll have to bandage it." His mother brought a first-aid box from the cabinet by the sink. "Tch! I've no wide bandages. Hold still!"

Gwyn hopped from foot to foot. Things took so long when you needed to be finished with them.

"What's your hurry, boy?" His mother spread yellow cream on the torn nail and began to wrap it up. "Anyone would think there was a time bomb here!"

Perhaps there is, sort of, Gwyn thought.

The bandage swelled into a giant grub.

His father peered in through the window. He tapped a pane. "I'm off to Pendewi, Gwyn. Want to come?"

"I . . . well . . ." Was it here, or was it there that he was needed?

"Make up your mind, boy. I'm late as it is!" Mr. Griffiths vanished.

"Go on, Gwyn. Go and see Alun." His mother pushed him gently away.

The Land Rover hustled noisily from the lane.

Gwyn hovered by the door. "OK," he said and rushed through it. He needed to talk to someone.

As he flung himself onto the seat beside his father, he realized it was not Alun he wanted to see, but Nia, Alun's sister.

Alun was a good friend and would be, probably, forever, but he drew away from magic and all talk of it. Only Nia understood. Only she had glimpsed events beyond the world that surrounded her and welcomed spells as naturally as she did spring flowers.

The journey to Pendewi took twenty minutes. It would have taken ten if the lane had not been so steep. The town was only five miles away. But the Griffiths's farm was the highest on the mountain. It lay at the end of a track that was hardly more than a twisting channel carved into the rock. Even in the Land Rover, progress was slow until they reached the main road. Then it was a few minutes of racing with coast-bound cars and trailers, over a bridge and down into the town.

Traffic between the Lloyds and the Griffithses was frequent. They had been neighbors until the mountain drove the Lloyds down to the valley. Its pitiless winters had been too much for Iestyn Lloyd, father of eight. Such a man must be master of his home so he had left farming and sold his old house to Gwyn's Uncle Idris. Now Iestyn was a butcher in Pendewi and doing very nicely. But five miles and a different way of life could not interrupt a friendship that was as constant as time.

The Lloyds lived at number six High Street. Their tall terraced house had two doors, one blue for the shop, the other black for the family. Gwyn and his father went into the shop. Iestyn was placing chickens onto shiny trays in the window. "Alun's not here," he told Gwyn. "Gone swimming with the twins."

"Doesn't matter," Gwyn said.

"Wife's out, too, showing the baby off again!" Iestyn gave a smug wink.

"I'll go and see Nia!"

Leaving the men to discuss the price of lamb, Gwyn turned through a door that led into the house beyond — the Lloyds' living quarters.

It was a rare, quiet moment in a house that held eight children.

Gwyn walked down the passage to the open back door, but he did not step into what they called the yard, a small square of dry grass confined by ivy-covered walls and the back of the house. In one wall a glass pane revealed scarlet carcasses hanging in the butcher's room. And beside the low wall that held the garden back from the river, Nia had planted bright flowers, almost, it seemed, as a distraction from the lifeless gaudy things behind her father's window.

Today, however, the distraction came from elsewhere. The boys had made a hammock and slung it between the branches of the next door neighbor's apple tree. They had tied rope and twine and their mother's rags into a bright lattice, and where the rags were knotted, thin strips of color floated like tiny breeze-blown flags.

Catrin was lying in the hammock while Iolo, who was eight, gently set the swing in motion.

Catrin was sixteen; she had cornflower blue eyes and abundant blond hair. Gwyn thought she was probably the most beautiful girl in Wales. Lately he had found it difficult to talk to her. He did not even come up to her shoulder.

Catrin turned and waved. She looked like a princess, swinging in a basket of silk ribbons.

"I'm looking for Nia," Gwyn mumbled and stepped back into the passage. He could hear voices at the top of the house, Nerys and Nia arguing.

He walked to the bottom of the stairs but decided against interrupting.

The shouting subsided. A door slammed.

Gwyn sank onto the only seat in the hall, a low oak box where outgrown boots and shoes waited for the next child to find and approve them.

The hall was cool and shady. Gwyn expected to be soothed, but if anything his agitation increased.

Could it be here, the menace that was troubling his hands? Surely nothing could invade this cozy house. It was too crammed with children; it was barricaded with noise, constant movement, and the smell of washing. Could a demon slip through a swinging door or slide in on a draft beneath loose windows? And if so, where could it hide? None of the small low-beamed rooms was empty for long.

Gwyn hummed tunelessly.

And then, from the top of a bookcase, the telephone rang shrilly. He stared at the instrument, vibrating on its perch, hoping that someone would come to put it out of its misery. Perhaps he should answer it? Take a message? But he found that he couldn't touch it. He was about to escape through the front door when Iolo bounded in exclaiming, "Is it for me? I bet it is! My friend said he'd call."

Perhaps Iolo was too eager, for the receiver slipped out of his hand and swung on its black cord, back and forth across the dusty books. For some reason Iolo couldn't touch it, either. He shrank from it as a voice called from the instrument, "Who is there? Who is there?" And Nia ran down the stairs.

Taking in the scene she stepped toward the telephone ready for conversation, but suddenly she recoiled. And still the receiver swung on its shiny cord, impelled by nothing, unless it was the voice tumbling through it.

All three watched it helplessly, until it came to rest and then words spilled toward the reluctant children, clear and strong: a man's voice, deep and anxious, "Who is there? Who is there?"

It was only a voice but, somehow, it was as potent as electricity, and Gwyn was reminded of a black snake he'd heard of, very small and unremarkable, but with enough venom in its fangs to kill an army.

Gwyn clasped his hands and leaned over them as little stabs of pain shot through his fingers right up to his elbows.

"What've you done to your thumb?" Nia inquired, glad to find a reason for ignoring the voice.

"Been clumsy again," he said.

Catrin came into the hall. "What's the matter with you three?" she asked. "There's someone on the phone," and without waiting for them to reply she took the receiver and said, "Catrin Lloyd here! Who is it you want?" Her hair was all tangled gold from the swing.

"Catrin?" Gwyn could hear the voice. "Ah, Catrin," and it seemed to sigh. "It's Evan here. Your cousin Evan Llŷr!"

"Evan Llŷr!" Catrin repeated the name, frowning.

"You remember me?"

"I . . . I remember . . ."

"I don't believe you do." Here, a deep laugh. "It's been ten years, and you were a little child."

"I was six."

"How many of you are there now?"

"Eight."

"Eight?" There was an exclamation and a sentence inaudible to the listeners, except the words, ". . . and you're the oldest?"

"No, there's Nerys."

The voice softened, its words maddeningly muffled.

"You're coming here?" Catrin said.

Gwyn didn't like the way she pulled at her tangled curls, as though the voice was watching her.

"No, Mom's not at home . . . I'll tell her . . . Evan Llŷr is on his way. . . . Oh, you'll be welcome, sure. . . ." Catrin's free hand was at her throat, the other gripped the receiver.

They were only words, ordinary, pleasant words spoken far away but they slid through the air like a spell.

Gwyn wanted to shout, "Leave! Run, before he catches you!"

"Good-bye, now!" Catrin replaced the receiver. Her cheeks were pink. It could have been the heat. "You're a funny bunch," she said. "Why didn't you answer the poor man?"

"It wasn't for us," Nia said illogically.

"You can take messages, can't you?"

Nia chewed her lip but was not put down. "Not that kind," she muttered.

"Sometimes you're very silly!" Catrin swung away and ran up the stairs. Her feet were bare and her swirling skirt made mysterious shadows on her long golden legs.

Gwyn, watching Catrin, knew that Nia was watching him. He had never heard these two sisters quarrel. Nia had come off badly. Nerys could scold, and did, often. Catrin was always kind.

Remembering the scene, weeks later, Gwyn wondered if that was when the trouble began.

Iolo ran back outside, leaving Gwyn and Nia alone. Nia was distressed, and Gwyn didn't know how to comfort her. He had wanted to see her but the disembodied voice had confused him and he couldn't remember his purpose.

"I wish I could grow," he suddenly confided.

"Grow?" Nia said, as though the word had no meaning.

"You can't say you haven't noticed. Alun's much taller than me now."

"Alun's taller than everyone."

"Sometimes I think I'll never grow again," Gwyn rambled on, almost to himself. "I'll be a dwarf with thoughts rattling in my brain beside the magic and I'll never get clear of it."

"You'll grow," Nia said. It sounded automatic. She was still not herself.

"You coming, boy?" His father emerged through a door from the butcher's shop. He was carrying a package of meat, several red-stained bags, and the Lloyds' evening paper.

"Yes, Dad!" Gwyn pushed himself up from the chest. The tingling in his hands had eased. All at once he realized it was he who had, somehow, prevented Nia and Iolo from touching the telephone, and he didn't know why. *But whoever he is, this Evan Llŷr,* Gwyn thought, *he has already reached Catrin and I can't fix that.*

He followed his father to the front door but before leaving he turned to Nia and asked, "Are you all right?" He spoke softly, not wishing to call attention to his concern for the girl.

Nia nodded and replied, "Mind your fingers."

He knew she was not referring to his injured thumb. She understood. Nia, too, experienced irrational stabs of fear.

At least they had each other.

Something had invaded the house. They didn't know what it was, but it still smoldered there.

❊ ❊ ❊

Mr. Griffiths did not drive straight home. He pulled up where the mountain lane began to twist through arches of yellowing ash trees. The Land Rover lurched onto a bank that had become part of the crumbling wall it supported. Beyond the wall a cottage could be glimpsed, through a jungle of giant shrubs and plants.

"I've got Nain's bacon here," Mr. Griffith said. "Coming in to see her?"

"No," Gwyn replied.

"What's wrong, boy? Why do you keep avoiding your grandmother? What's the trouble between you?"

"No trouble, Dad." Gwyn drew himself into the back of the seat. "I just don't want to go in."

"Don't hurt her feelings! It's not much to ask, a quick visit, only take five minutes." Mr. Griffiths opened the door and looked hopefully at his son. "You were once so close, Gwyn, but you haven't visited her for weeks."

"No need to tell her I'm here," Gwyn said.

His father left him in peace. Gwyn watched him gradually disappear into the ocean of plants. He couldn't see the front door anymore.

Ashamed and angry with himself, Gwyn huddled down into his seat. His grandmother had a peephole through the plants, he knew, because once he'd been on the other side of her narrow window and seen his father herding his black cows up the lane.

He couldn't go in there anymore. Nain asked too much of him. Four years ago, on his ninth birthday, his grandmother had given him five gifts that had changed his life. For with the gifts had come the knowledge that he was a descendant of Gwydion, the magician, and inheritor of his power. Gwydion, who sent messages like fire in his fingers, who drew a force from him that could even search the stars.

Once Gwyn had been so triumphant, so proud of his talent, but being different led to loneliness. He had to watch himself, to curb his anger for fear of hurting others. Being extraordinary was not a happy state.

But wrapped in her dark, herbal-scented house, Nain always wanted more from him. Her own great-great-grandmother had been a witch, but she herself didn't have the power, so she wanted his, even when there was nothing to be done. She couldn't see that it was stunting him — Nain was as tall as her own front door.

One of those birthday gifts was a small carving of a mutilated horse that Gwyn must never use, nor leave where it might tempt a stranger to set it free, for it held the spirit of a demon prince. Gwyn's fingers burned again and he exclaimed aloud in surprise, wondering why he remembered the Lloyds' telephone when he thought of the broken horse, and why he heard the disembodied voice crying, "Who is there?"

Mr. Griffiths appeared at the gate. He looked grim. When he had climbed in beside Gwyn he said, "She knew you were here. It's cruel not to see her."

"I'm sorry!" He could not explain the reason to his father. Gwyn remained in his mute huddle.

His silence infuriated his father. "I won't force you, Gwyn, you know that," Mr. Griffiths spoke quietly at first and then he suddenly railed, "but, by God, you're a mean-spirited little beast!"

And you're a terror for losing your temper, Gwyn thought, but he said nothing.

Mr. Griffiths wrenched the hand brake free and jabbed at the ignition. The Land Rover rocked off the bank and roared up the lane, its occupants divided by an unwelcome quarrel.

The kitchen table was laid for dinner when they reached home. Cans, bowls, and messy ingredients had vanished.

"A genius you are, Glenys," Ivor Griffiths told his wife.

Rows of cakes in plastic wrap were stacked on the counter, neat as soldiers on parade.

"Wow!" breathed Gwyn. "You'll break a record with all this!"

His mother beamed and served the food, so Gwyn couldn't be rude and run upstairs just then. He knew now why he'd slipped a chisel into his pocket.

His father relaxed after his meal. He sat in his big armchair and read Iestyn Lloyd's newspaper.

Gwyn went up to his room. He stared at the rug beside his bed for a full minute, then he rolled it up, revealing five dusty floorboards. The center board had been replaced long ago by three short planks, one only half a yard long. The nails securing this board were obvious and shiny; they were only four years old. The others, scattered across the floor, brown and invisible, were more than two hundred.

Gwyn eased his chisel into a narrow gap at one end of the short board and began to wedge it up, wondering as he worked why he was invading the hiding place. Was it only for reassurance? The thing that he'd imprisoned there four years ago could surely not have escaped.

It was easier than he had imagined. Two nails suddenly

snapped free, then the others. The board was loose. Gently, Gwyn lifted it away.

Dust covered the hidden object in a thin gray film but did not conceal it. He experienced a tiny jolt of fear, but forced himself to bring into the light a small four-legged wooden creature.

He blew the dust away and it drifted into the warm air, some settling on his hands. It was smaller than he remembered and even more hideous — a mockery of a horse, with severed ears and tail, blank lidless eyes, and teeth bared forever in what could only be despair.

And Gwyn felt pity as he had four years before and a longing to do what he must never do — set the captured demon free and take away its pain. But the injunction still remained on a scrap of dappled paper tied to the creature's neck, "*Dim hon!* Not this!" scrawled in a witch's hand.

If he'd been rational then, he'd have replaced the horse in that safest of hiding places, but panic and his aching fingers distracted him, caused him to hover about the room, rumbling in drawers and cupboards. At length he chose a beam set high into the back wall but protruding twenty inches from it; a narrow shelf where he kept his most precious possessions.

He climbed onto the bed and pushed the horse between a lump of glittering quartz and a crowd of pearly shells. The other gifts were there, too: the yellow scarf, folded tight; a dry stick of seaweed; and the pipe that his ancestors had flung to Gwyn through time so that he might hear voices inaudible to other mortals. Once, he'd heard a sound he wished he could forget.

The last gift was resting in a tiny circle of gossamer at the end of the beam: Arianwen, the spider, sent by his lost sister from another world, in exchange for an ancient metal brooch.

"What d'you think, Arianwen?" Gwyn spread his fingers invitingly along the beam. "Will I grow? Is the magic shrinking me? I'm tired of it, see. It hurts. I don't want it anymore!"

The spider crept toward him, and as she moved into deep shadow beneath the beam, a cloud of glowing particles spiraled around her.

Gwyn took her into his hand. "There," he said, "I didn't mean it!" She was part of the magic, and he would never reject her. He could hardly feel her, but the coolness of her silvery body soothed his tingling fingers.

Gently he dropped her onto the broken horse. "Guard it for a while," he said. "I don't know what to do."

But the little spider ran away from the dark creature, and Gwyn couldn't blame her. Something writhed in there, someone glared out from the dead eyes: a mad, imprisoned prince. But what did it have to do with that lost voice clutching at Catrin through a telephone receiver?

Gwyn stepped away and jumped off his bed. "I'm not sleeping with you there," he told the horse. "I'll move you later." He left the room, closing the door tight.

Behind the horse's terrible injuries, someone smiled to himself. He had waited for two thousand years — what did a few days matter? The man he had summoned was drawing closer.

CHAPTER TWO

The Wounded Soldier

CATRIN WITHHELD THE MESSAGE. IT WAS THE BEGINNING OF a time when she was to keep more and more of herself away from her family.

It isn't my message, Nia thought. *It isn't mine to pass on.* Perhaps there was no telephone call. She didn't want to think about the lost voice stealing into the house and catching at her sister. If she had answered the phone, the message and the voice would have been hers, but Gwyn Griffiths had come between her and Evan Llŷr. She knew it was Gwyn, sitting there, bent over his fingers like the wizard he was. He had done it before. She knew the feeling now; he had stopped her from doing things, saved her! He hadn't stopped Catrin, though!

When the letter came, two days later, Mrs. Lloyd was unprepared and quite flustered at the news. "Evan Llŷr!" she exclaimed over the buzz of eight children munching breakfast. Her voice had such an unnatural ring it managed to penetrate the noise and even to subdue it.

"Who is Evan Llŷr, Mom?" Nerys asked.

"Your cousin!"

"Our cousins are girls," said Gareth, grimacing.

"Rotten girls," Siôn repeated, always mean-spirited where the opposite sex was concerned.

"He says he telephoned," Mrs. Lloyd went on, ignoring the twins. "Gave someone a message!"

"I forgot," said Catrin, vigorously buttering her toast. "I'm sorry."

You didn't forget, Nia thought. *You wanted to keep it all to yourself, Catrin Lloyd.*

"He wants to come . . . dear, dear . . . I wish I'd known . . . well, of course." Mrs. Lloyd brought the letter closer to her face.

Nia leaned over the table for the butter dish and peered into Catrin's face.

"Don't look at me like that," Catrin said sharply. "I forgot. Why didn't you remind me?"

"It wasn't my message, and anyway, how was I to know you'd keep it to yourself?"

"Oh, no . . . and he's been wounded!" Mrs. Lloyd announced.

"Wounded?" The twins looked up.

"Yes, wounded. He's a soldier, didn't I tell you?"

"A soldier?" Three boys brightened at the word.

"I can hardly read this part . . ." Mrs. Lloyd ran her fingers through her uncombed morning curls.

Nia abandoned her breakfast and ran behind her mother. It was strange to read the handwriting that belonged to that deep disturbing voice. Gwyn wasn't there, this time, to keep Evan Llŷr from reaching her.

The letter was written in black ink. At the top of the paper the words sprawled huge and forceful toward the right hand margin, but after a few sentences the character of the writing changed, it dwindled as though the writer had lost confidence; either the ink was not flowing or the pen was hardly touching the paper. And through and around the uneven, hesitant pattern of lines, Nia caught something of the unknown cousin behind them and was, at the same time, entranced and infinitely saddened. The words at the end could hardly be deciphered: "Forgive me; if you've no room, I'll go elsewhere."

"No 'Love from,'" Nerys remarked. "Do we really know this man?"

"Anyone would think he was a stranger," muttered her mother. "Of course we know him, though it's been ten years, and of course he can come. There's a bit of space in Iolo's room." Then she dropped the letter on the table and exclaimed, "Oh, but he wants peace, and it's such a tiny room. He must have a place to himself."

"Iolo can come in with Bethan and me," Nia offered.

"No!" moaned Iolo.

"Please, dear. I'm sure it won't be for long," Mrs. Lloyd gave Iolo one of her special winning smiles. "It'll be nice, three quiet ones together!"

"And three noisy ones down below," said Nia. She wouldn't have shared her room with Alun or the twins.

"It's half past eight," Mr. Lloyd informed his children from the kitchen door. "You'll be late for school, get on with it. Betty, those boys haven't even brushed their hair."

"I got a letter, Iestyn," Mrs. Lloyd jumped up guiltily, "from Evan. You remember, Evan Llŷr."

"I remember," said Iestyn, none too warmly.

"He's coming here!"

"Is he now?"

All at once, hairbrushing conveniently forgotten, the kitchen was full of boys' excited questions. "Would Iolo's room be large enough for a soldier? Where would his boots go? Would there be weapons under the bed?"

"Not if I've got anything to say about it!" Mr. Lloyd might be a butcher, but his lust for blood did not extend beyond his trade. He regarded soldiery with suspicion. "Now, up those stairs and clean yourselves up!"

So the children had to wait until dinnertime before they could squeeze further information from their mother.

"Who is Evan, really?" Nia asked for the second time.

"I've told you, my brother's son," her mother sighed patiently.

That was no answer. "Yes, but who . . . ?" Nia persisted.

"I'll tell you." Mrs. Lloyd, easier now that all ten plates were filled, sat down and embarked on a history of the Llŷrs, past and present. "As you know, there were three of us girls: Auntie Megan, Auntie Cath, and me. Well, I was the youngest and your Uncle Dai was fifteen years older. He was a half brother, my mother's child but not my father's!"

"So he's not a Llŷr!" Nerys put in.

"Well . . . no . . ."

"Neither is Evan!" Nerys went on. She was always one for grabbing at little details. She liked stories to be neat.

Her mother didn't want to linger on complications but she knew Nerys would give her no peace until she had every piece of the puzzle. "Dai was only a baby when my parents married," she explained, "so my father adopted him legally, and gave him his name."

"Who was Dai's father then?" Nia asked.

"I don't know!" Mrs. Lloyd seemed surprised by her own answer. "I never knew. I never asked."

This piece of information fascinated Nia.

So there's a part of Evan that we'll never know about, she thought. Aloud she said, "Go on about Uncle Dai."

Relieved to have got off lightly this time, Mrs. Lloyd continued, "Well, Dai never did like farming, so he went off to work in the bank, in Wrexham. Did very well, too. Must have been quite a catch in those days. He was handsome, too, your Uncle Dai."

"What's a catch?" asked Iolo, grasping at the only point of interest in his mother's story.

"Like a fish," Alun said quickly.

"Is he dead, then?" Iolo inquired.

"Dead? Why should he be dead?" Mrs. Lloyd was in danger of losing her train of thought.

"He means like a fish being caught." Nia cheerfully came to the rescue.

"I do not!" Iolo said indignantly. "You said *was*, Mom. You said he *was* handsome!"

"Oh, in those days. He's quite old now."

"Where is he?" Nia asked.

"Where? In Australia. Where was I?" Mrs. Lloyd looked at

her oldest daughter. Nerys could usually be relied upon at such times, but she was polishing her eyeglasses. Catrin was gazing into a space that was probably occupied, Nia thought, by a boy on a black horse. Catrin was in love with Michael McGoohan, the doctor's son.

But Nia had not lost the thread of the story. "Uncle Dai, who was handsome and rich because of being a bank manager, went to Australia," she said. "But what about Evan?"

"There were two of them," Mrs. Lloyd said absently, then all at once she seemed to regret having launched herself thus far.

"Two what?" Nia prompted eagerly.

"Evan had an older brother, Emrys, but he died when he was only eight." Mrs. Lloyd disclosed this sad and dreadful fact as though she intended to end her story there, and for most of her family it had the desired effect. The awfulness of dying when you were eight had to be respected in silence.

The twins managed a mumbled "Aw!" and glanced at Iolo, but Nia needed to know more about the survivor. "And then what?" she asked.

"Then what? Then what?" Mr. Lloyd mimicked irritably. "It's like a pound of flesh you're wanting, Nia Lloyd. Haven't you had enough Llŷr history?" It was clear that he had had too much; his own family was not so numerous nor as interesting as his wife's.

"But I want to know about Evan," Nia stubbornly persisted.

"Go on, then! Go on, Betty! I'll get my own cup of tea!" Mr. Lloyd made a great to-do about squeezing himself out of his chair at the end of the table.

"Sit down, Da," said Nerys, reaching for his cup.

"And go on, Mom," said Nia. "Emrys died and then what?"

"Then, sometime after, your aunt and uncle went to Australia, but Evan wouldn't go. He wanted to be a soldier."

"A soldier, and he's coming here," the twins yelled at each other.

"A soldier, yes, but one that's been to college." Mrs. Lloyd was proud of her nephew. "Oh, he was bright, that Evan. He's a major now, it seems, and still only in his thirties."

"He's getting on, then." Nia began to be disappointed.

"He's younger than I am," her mother laughed. She wasn't old, Nia thought. Her curls were still golden-brown and her eyes as blue as Catrin's.

"But for a cousin he's old," Iolo said. "I mean, he's past playing, isn't he?"

"He's a soldier," scoffed Gareth.

"A fighter," added Siôn.

"Yes," Iolo sadly agreed. He lived in the hope of finding someone who would play his games with him. His older brothers were into violent activities where he was always the victim.

"There was another side to Evan, as I remember," Mrs. Lloyd told Iolo, but she refused to talk any further.

When dinner was over, and Catrin had carried Bethan away for her bath, Nia surprised her family by demanding to take Alun's turn with the dish drying. She wanted to be alone with her mother.

"What was on the other side, Mom?" Nia probed while she gently dried her father's favorite mug.

"Other side of what, dear?" Mrs. Lloyd was thinking of beds now.

"You said there was another side to Evan Llŷr."

"Yes." Mrs. Lloyd became suddenly wary. "Well — I meant he wasn't all soldier." She caught sight of the kitchen clock. "Is that the time? I want to watch the news!" She peeled off her rubber gloves and left the kitchen for the front room.

Nia dogged her. She wasn't going to let it go at that.

The news hadn't started. They remembered the kitchen clock was ten minutes fast. Mrs. Lloyd switched the TV off. She sank onto the sofa and drummed her fingers on one arm. Nia wriggled in beside her.

"Go on about Evan, Mom!"

"What do you . . ." Mrs. Lloyd began and then something caught her eye in the street beyond the lace curtain.

A horse and rider came into view. The horse was huge and glossy black, the young man on his back had attractive, youthfully rounded features, thick brown hair that curled over his collar, and skin that seemed permanently flushed, giving him the appearance of someone always on the edge of a violent emotion.

The sight of the boy and the horse seemed to irritate Mrs. Lloyd. "That Michael McGoohan," she muttered. "Thinks he's so great, doesn't he, loafing around on a big black horse."

"You can't loaf on a horse, Mom," Nia said. "Anyway, they ride horses a lot in Ireland." She felt she had to defend Catrin's interest. "They think nothing of it."

"Why doesn't he get a job? He left school."

"He's waiting for the right one. Catrin likes him."

"I know. She could do better!"

Michael McGoohan glanced toward their window, hoping perhaps for a glimpse of Catrin. Nia and her mother, safely concealed behind the lace, stared out at him. The young man looked up and scanned the second-floor windows. Disappointed, he moved his horse on.

Nia waited until the rhythm of hoofbeats had receded then prodded her mother. "Mom, about Emrys. How did he die?"

"Oh, Nia." Betty Lloyd gave a long, sad sigh. "I've kept it to myself for so long. It's something I'd like to forget."

"No one else knows, then?"

"Of course they do. When a boy dies, people have to know. You can't keep it a secret." She took a breath. "He fell out of a tree. There!"

Nia had annoyed her mother, and it was the last thing she'd intended. But she felt compelled to pursue the subject. If she let go of it now, she would never know the story as it should be known.

"Oh Mom, please tell," she begged. "I know that isn't all of it. It can't be. There's more. The part that hurts you."

Mrs. Lloyd gripped the arm of the sofa. Nia thought she'd pushed too far and that her mother was going to fling away the subject of Evan and Emrys in favor of the television news. Then Mrs. Lloyd relaxed; she put her arm round Nia and said, "Emrys was the one we watched. The one everyone loved for his brave ways. Evan was quiet — a kind little boy, always behind Emrys, always following, and a bit of a coward. Emrys loved to climb trees. Evan would watch, too frightened to climb, and Emrys would taunt him.

"They were gone a long time that day. It was autumn, the chestnuts were ripe. Emrys had climbed the chestnut tree to reach the best . . .

"I was sent out to find them. I was twelve. When I saw them I thought it was a bit of play-acting, but they were too quiet for that, and so still, and all at once I knew why. I'll never forget that day, not as long as I live. Evan never cried, see, not once, just walked away and left me calling to his mother. And the next day, when we were all wandering around, still shocked, I suppose, and hardly knowing what we were doing, he slipped out, that strange child, and climbed the very tree that had killed his brother, almost to the top. I followed him and waited till he came down, all serious-looking but somehow satisfied, and when I asked him, 'Why did you do that, Evan? How could you?' he just said, 'I climbed higher, Betty, higher than Emrys.'

"I thought he'd lost his mind and must have shown what I thought because he put his arms so carefully around me and said, 'Don't cry, Betty, Evan is here!' He was so gentle."

Betty Lloyd had never spoken about the past at such length. Perhaps it was because she had been able to sweep her daughter into the hours that still startled her when she remembered them. And now Nia, too, saw the fierce dead boy, and the gentle one beside, unable to cry.

"He came again, often," Mrs. Lloyd went on. "I don't think his parents understood him anymore. He came every summer. Long summers they were, and always hot, as I remember, and this will sound heartless to you, but we didn't miss Emrys anymore."

❊ ❊ ❊

So Nia thought she knew all about Evan Llŷr. She'd heard his voice, seen his letter, knew his childhood. She believed she was armed against whatever it was that Gwyn Griffiths wished to save her from.

The weather broke at last. A wind swept down from the mountains and blasted arctic wet into the valley. Chimneys toppled, and the trees flung ripe fruit and fading leaves over the sodden fields. The river rose and spilled into basements and backyards. It had happened before and would do so again.

For two days, inky black clouds threatened with thunder. Roads became muddy torrents of debris. The wind screamed past electric poles, snapped at hedges, gleefully toyed with loose bricks and trash cans. Traffic was diverted and Pendewi would have been a quiet place if it hadn't been for the wind.

The prince still came, though later than expected, so the boys were into their noisy after dinnertime, and Mrs. Lloyd was busy with Nerys in the kitchen. It was Nia who answered the door. She opened it very slowly and carefully; even so, she was unprepared.

Evan Llŷr was tall, but not in uniform as Nia had expected. He wore a dark sweater and jeans and something flung around his shoulders in the manner of a cloak. His appearance caused a jolt in Nia's mind, and the reception she'd intended became disorganized. "Aw," she mumbled. "Is it . . . are you?"

"Hello!" said Evan Llŷr.

And Nia could not reply to this because, in all her eleven years, she had never been alone with anyone so startlingly handsome. Black wing eyebrows accentuated a brilliant blue gaze; abundant black hair sprang away from fine aquiline features and the faintest of blue shadows echoed the long curves of his upper lip. Evan Llŷr was the prince from every fairy tale; he was fierce and kind — and immensely troubled.

"I'm Evan Llŷr," he said.

"I know," Nia opened the door wider.

Her prince smiled and Nia felt so small she wondered if he could really see her.

They stood a moment regarding each other, a moment in which Nia came to know her cousin more intimately than in all the later hours of close conversation.

And she was still standing there, wondering at the intense and unfamiliar sensation, when her mother came up behind her exclaiming, "Nia . . . Nia, what are you doing, girl? Let the man in . . . is it? It is, it's Evan!"

And then the prince was walking past Nia, and there were boys whooping down the stairs, and her mother was bouncing like a girl and planting sugary kisses on the noble cheekbone.

Nia turned from these intimacies to close the front door and as she did so, noticed something black and bronze in the misty road, steaming like a tired beast. Such a car did not seem appropriate for a prince, but more the sort of vehicle a demon would choose.

She followed the company into the kitchen where her father gave Evan Llŷr his own seat at the head of the table. But it didn't seem right that a prince should be sitting there, with clutter and crumbs still on the cloth, with sticky jars on the dresser and stained dish towels hanging on the door.

He seemed happy with all this, however; a plate of stew piping hot and a glass of plum wine, the last bottle, kept especially for such an occasion.

Between mouthfuls the new cousin made up for lost years: counted heads, repeated names, and asked all the questions expected of a long-absent relative. And although someone was missing he never mentioned it, but turned his head very slightly, now and again, to listen to the sonata that Catrin was playing in the room beyond.

No one could stem the twins' eager curiosity. What weapons did a major use? How many men did he lead? When was he wounded and how? The soldier parried these questions gently, some he answered, some he left, and then Gareth asked, "How many men have you killed, Cousin Evan?"

And Nia noticed a sudden stillness fall about Evan. He seemed to depart from them. His fingers tightened around the cut-glass tumbler, then abandoned it. And he withdrew a shaking hand into safe shadows beneath the table.

"How many?" Siôn pressed.

"Leave Evan in peace, boys," Mrs. Lloyd said in what seemed to Nia a meaningless way, for her mother was beside herself with a sort of silly excitement.

"You're no different, Betty," Evan remarked, almost himself again. "Last time I saw you on the lane from Tŷ Llŷr you had a baby in your arms. It's the same now, and you're the same."

"Don't tease, Evan!" Betty Lloyd blushed, although she was a few years older than the soldier, and pressed her face into Bethan's dark curls. "It's ten years, Nia was the baby then."

For a moment Nia had her cousin's undivided attention and then someone came into the room behind her and took her moment away. Nia, watching closely, saw a hint of dismay and then confusion in Evan's dark blue eyes.

"And this is Catrin," Mrs. Lloyd said.

Catrin walked into a space where the light was brightest. Her hair shone as though she had brushed it a thousand times, just for the occasion. But she looked nervous and unsure.

Evan smiled. "The musician," he said quietly.

"Catrin took your message," Mrs. Lloyd told him, "but she kept it to herself," and she immediately tried to make light of her remark by giving a diffident laugh.

She is aware of something, Nia thought, *and so am I, and so is Catrin. We have changed, each one of us, but we won't speak about it, not yet. All this happened before, long, long ago; it's like a story being retold. But how are we going to find the way to a happy ending?*

CHAPTER THREE
A Spirit Freed

"HE'S COME THEN, ALUN'S SOLDIER COUSIN?" SAID GWYN'S mother. She'd been toiling away at the new stove, a French contraption that heated radiators and served as a boiler as well as doing the cooking. Gradually, Glenys Griffiths was dragging her reluctant husband into the twenty-first century.

There was a glass oven door in the new stove; Mrs. Griffiths could see the bread, and it wasn't rising. You couldn't bake bread, it seemed, when it was heating the radiators.

"He came," Gwyn said. "Alun says he's not like a soldier. Won't talk about the army, or anything like that."

"Just as well!" Mrs. Griffiths flung herself back into an easy chair. "I thought that storm would blow the heat away but it seems to be back, just as close, and it's nearly October."

"He wants to come and see Tŷ Llŷr, this Evan," Gwyn said. "They're bringing him up this afternoon. Think I'll go and have a look at him."

"Have a look?" his mother smiled. "Sounds like he's a toy soldier."

"You know what I mean. Can I bring him back for a snack?"

"How many? There'll be no bread." Mrs. Griffiths glanced ruefully at the oven.

"Cake then. I don't know how many. Maybe the soldier will want to stay at Tŷ Llŷr. He loves that place, Alun says."

"I remember him," Gwyn's mother disclosed with a coy and unfamiliar expression. "A tall young man, quiet, with eyes like — the summer sea." Memories of Evan released the poet in her, it seemed.

"He used to come and help the Lloyds at lambing time," Glenys continued. "He was good, too, up all hours, out in all weather, never complained. He didn't get on with Alun's dad, though, I don't know why. He'd have been good on a farm, shame there was no place for him."

"Sounds drastic to be a soldier instead," Gwyn remarked. "Like going in the wrong direction."

"Well, he was strange, too!"

Gwyn knew that. He'd heard the voice reaching into Nia's home. "I'll try and bring him back, then," he told his mother. "So you can look into his sea-blue eyes!"

"Gwyn!" Was it the heat or did she blush?

"It'd better be a great cake," he teased and leaped away from his confused mother, closing the door against her muttered protestations.

He decided against walking down the lane. His grandmother might be in her front yard and he was still not ready for a discussion. So, feeling a little foolish, he walked through the farmyard and climbed the gate. The twine that secured the broken bolt would take too long to unravel.

Wishing he did not feel so furtive and ill at ease on his own territory, he walked around the back of the outbuildings and then downhill, through two fields of sheep. There was a shaggy little horned ram in the second field. He stared at Gwyn with his sharp hazel-colored eyes and moved protectively along the ranks of ewes until the boy had left his field.

Gwyn scrambled over a stone wall and dropped onto Nain's ground. The wild acre behind his grandmother's cottage was choked with weeds — burdock and thistles crawled around giant artichokes, comfrey, and borage. None of this was accidental, nor was it a "crime" as Iestyn Lloyd would have it. "It's a prime bit of pasture and she's let it go," he would complain. But Gwyn knew that every inch was planned, every plant known. Birds flocked to Rhiannon Griffiths's fruitful meadow, bees found untainted pollen there, ladybugs thrived, and rodents happily multiplied.

"Everything has its use," Rhiannon would say, "and there's a cure for all ills in the things that spring from the earth!"

And Gwyn knew that his grandmother was not crazy. He also knew that none of her herbs would solve his problem. They would not help him grow or stop the burning in his hands. He needed something else — something or someone?

He passed the grove of ash trees that separated the weeds from his grandmother's more formal herb garden. The feathery leaves were already yellowing in the dry weather. Nain loved the ash above all trees. Gwyn dared not look toward the cottage, but couldn't resist a guilty glance at the garden where he suddenly became aware that he was looking straight at his grandmother, who was staring at him. She'd been so still, wrapped in a green shawl and kneeling on the path, he hadn't noticed her at first.

Gwyn started, then smiled. It was too late to run away. She didn't speak, didn't move.

"Hello, Nain!" he said at last, and his voice sounded withered and unwilling.

His grandmother looked away from him. She was holding a trowel that she began to poke into the dry soil. When she spoke she seemed to be addressing the earth. "Snooping are we, Gwydion Gwyn?" she said.

"No, not snooping, Nain," he said.

"Why didn't you come to the door, then, instead of lurking in my garden like a thief?"

"I wasn't lurking, Nain. I was just passing," he said huffily. He felt silly peering through the sprays of colored leaves.

"I see. Not coming to see *me*, then!"

"Well . . ." he shifted from one foot to the other.

"So run along, then," she said coldly. "Don't let me detain you from your urgent business."

All at once Gwyn felt that he should speak to his grandmother.

It wasn't pity that led him to her at last. He went to seek her advice, to arm himself with a little of her ancient wisdom before facing the owner of that dark and worrying voice.

He sidled past the trees and walked up the path. When he was standing beside her, he said, "I'm going to see that soldier."

"Soldier?" She was too obviously casual to be uninterested.

"You must have heard," he said. "The Lloyds' cousin. He was wounded in Belfast."

"That one!"

He could tell, in spite of her digging away at the earth, that she was profoundly interested. "Do you know him?" he asked. "He came to Tŷ Llŷr, when he was a boy, Alun says. Says he's not much of a soldier either, though he's a major and won medals."

"Poor creature," Nain said.

"Poor creature?" he repeated, surprised.

"That one, that soldier. Poor injured soul." She shook her head.

"Why poor, Nain? He's better." Gwyn was intrigued. What was she going on about now?

"Is he better? Is he?" She turned for the first time and darted a fierce black look up at her grandson. "Why has he come here, then?"

"To recover. There's no mystery!" He wished he could believe that himself.

"But why here, eh? After all this time?"

He wasn't sure whether she expected him to know the answer or was trying to kindle an interest. Couldn't she tell that he was already on his guard? "His relatives are here," Gwyn explained.

"It's not so simple, Gwydion Gwyn. It's not just his relatives. I know that man. And I knew he'd come back, to finish a story. Perhaps you can help him."

"Me?" He was genuinely astonished.

"Of course, you. Who else? You're the magician."

"Oh Nain, don't . . ." he groaned and kicked at the pebbles on the path.

"You can't just shake it off, boy. You're a magician. I'll shout it. Nothing you can do will unsay it." Nain stood up and clutched at his shoulder. She was such a tall woman. He felt buried in her shadow. "Listen, it isn't my fault. I didn't make you what you are. I just woke you up. And weren't you pleased, Gwydion Gwyn, when you discovered your power, and didn't it bring you joy to see your lost sister and to save your cousin Emlyn with a spell?"

"Yes, yes!" He shrugged her off and turned away. "But I don't want it anymore, see! I'm sick of it. It's making me tired!"

He began to run toward the trees but when he'd passed through the grove and couldn't see the tall figure on the path, the words he'd meant to keep to himself burst from him. "I want to grow!" he cried, and he tore through the wild acre as though every second he spent there would diminish him further.

But as he broke free of the giant weeds and tumbled onto smooth-cropped grass, he heard a voice singsonging after him. "You *will* grow, Gwydion Gwyn. You will, I promise you!"

He believed his grandmother, as he always had and always would, and rushed down toward the Tŷ Llŷr fields, feeling lighter and more hopeful than he'd done for many months.

❊ ❊ ❊

Ivor Griffiths now farmed the land that had once belonged to the Lloyds, but the ancient farmhouse was owned by Idris Llewelyn, the painter. The chapel where Idris worked was too small for his growing family, and ever since the fire there, four years earlier, his wife, Elinor, had refused to live in the place. Elinor and Gwyn's mother were sisters, and Gwyn now considered Tŷ Llŷr a second home. Nia, too, used it as a refuge; it was the only house where she felt truly at peace. In fact there was an embracing atmosphere about Tŷ Llŷr that suggested it had been the site of a well-loved home even before the present farmhouse had been built. And so it had become a meeting place, where children from three families would come to find one another and discuss their problems.

A stream ran past Tŷ Llŷr — a wild, rocky stream of clear water that sprang from the mountain summit and spilled in a silvery torrent beside the lane until it found the Lloyds' old farmhouse, perched on its granite rock, and there the water, seeking an easier passage, found soft shale that allowed it to meander gently around the back of the farmyard. The bank, here, was formed from the roots of willow and alder; it was an untidy network that twisted and curled into the riverbed.

Gwyn found Evan Llŷr sitting on a wide rock, his feet supported by the trellis of blanched roots, with Nia and Iolo on either side of him. The man and the boy each held a string with a polished chestnut tied to the end. The chestnuts flew on their strings. They spun and cracked while the soldier issued instructions. "Keep the string short, Iolo! Hit it on the top, now. Harder! Ah, you've got me!"

Iolo laughed and Nia smiled; she watched the soldier, not the battling chestnuts, Gwyn noted. And then she saw him and exclaimed, "It's Gwyn!"

Gwyn faced the group across the stream. The soldier looked up, lifting his hand to shade his eyes from the sun. "So you're Gwyn Griffiths," he said, and there was nothing in his voice except a gentle curiosity.

Gwyn stepped into the stream, and the current pushed against him, little billows of shining spume lapping around the top of his boots.

"It's deep there," Nia shouted. "You'll get your socks wet."

But Gwyn took his time, feeling for the smooth higher pebbles with his feet. He paced slowly through the stream, watching his step, aware of a sea-blue glance marking him out, until he came within a yard of the bank and then he stopped and looked up at the trio.

Evan Llŷr regarded him eagerly, intrigued and puzzled, and for a moment, Gwyn was thrown off guard because the soldier's smile was so truly welcoming. And then he remembered the voice that had snaked through the air, repelling the same three people who now found its owner so irresistible. And Gwyn sensed a terrible contradiction. He was in the presence of something utterly unfamiliar. There was an emptiness about Evan Llŷr, a fearlessness that had nothing to do with courage, and it betrayed the kind and gentle smile.

Does he know who I am? Gwyn wondered.

"Here!" The soldier held out his hand and Gwyn accepted it. There was no warmth in the soldier's flesh, it was smooth and dry and his touch sent a tiny circuit of pain trickling through Gwyn, like a ghost. It was so fleeting Gwyn did not even gasp, but the soldier's hand tightened around his own and he was sure Evan knew what had happened between them.

"Don't fall," the soldier said.

And Gwyn replied, "It's my boots, they're slippery!" And as he clambered up beside Nia's cousin, he was baffled by a sense of being quite alone with Evan in a place where giant trees replaced the hedges and a midnight cloud obscured the sun.

"I won," Iolo shouted into the quietness. "Do you want to play, Gwyn?"

"No, not now," Gwyn said, trying to shake off unreality. "Got to get my hands in the right mood."

"Look!" Nia held out a handful of chestnuts. "Aren't they beautiful when they're new? There are hundreds this year, all over the lane, big and shiny."

Gwyn took the largest from her. It gleamed brown and velvet smooth; the underside was white and soft as down, just plucked from its shell. "I'd like to plant this at home," he said, "but it would die. It's too cold and high for chestnut trees. Nain says it's strange that a chestnut tree should grow on a mountain at all."

"It's in a sheltered spot," said Evan, "away from the north wind. The topsoil has collected there just so such a tree could thrive." And then he added, "I climbed that tree once, long ago."

Iolo began to attack the roots at his feet, but his victorious chestnut broke free of its string and bounced into the water. "Aw!" he cried. "My conqueror, he's gone," and he leaped up to follow the prizewinner downstream.

"Let it go, Iolo," Evan said, "and I'll get you another, an even greater winner."

"We're going for a walk," Nia reminded him. "You wanted to see the mountain again, you said."

"So I did, and so we shall." Evan got to his feet. "But I have forgotten the best way, so you'll have to keep close to me."

"We'll all go," Gwyn said. He felt protective toward the mountain. It was his place, his and his father's; it was Griffiths land right to the summit. "And we'll take Emlyn," he added when he saw his cousin, a tall boy with wild brown hair, coming through the yard.

"Take Emlyn where?" his cousin asked. "I'm busy."

"No, you're not." Gwyn winked slyly.

Emlyn showed no surprise. "Oh, I'm not," he said.

Gwyn knew he would help. They were as close and comfortable as brothers, even if Emlyn did not always understand how his cousin could sometimes ache with apprehension on a sunny day. Emlyn had no space to waste on the inexplicable, his mind was reserved for the animals he made. He already showed a considerable talent for wood-carving and it was clear that he would follow in his father's footsteps. His four-year-old brother, Geraint, on the other hand, longed only to be a farmer like his uncle Ivor.

In the end it was the four children who walked up the mountain leaving Evan Llŷr to follow, because Emlyn's mother came to her door and begged the soldier to stay for just one cup of tea. Mrs. Llewelyn was usually shy of strangers but the major had charmed her with his quiet diffidence. His request to wander through her yard had been so courteous, his smile so irresistible, she was eager to share more of her home with him and to show him around the places he had loved.

"I'll catch up to you," Evan told the children. "Wait for me at Tŷ Bryn."

So the children walked up to Gwyn's home where they visited the cat and her three white kittens lying in a barn. Then Gwyn mentioned the kite he had observed hovering over the lower mountains, and Nia couldn't wait to see it.

"We'll need binoculars," Gwyn said, "just to make sure. It might have been a buzzard, but I think it was too big, and the wings had touches of red."

"I'll get them," Iolo offered. Gwyn's attic, crammed with books and maps of the planets, was always worth a visit.

"They're hanging on my bed," Gwyn called after him. But Iolo knew exactly where to look.

He was away for some time. Gwyn would have gone after him, to see what he was up to, but Nia and Emlyn had already started up the mountain track. It was the sort of breezy day that seemed to forbid the indoors. It spun Gwyn through the farm-yard, infecting him with a reckless forgetfulness and leading him up the mountain away from the thing he should have remembered.

Inside Gwyn's room Iolo was reaching for the binoculars when a dark shape fluttered through the open window. It flipped over Iolo's head, knocked into a cupboard, and swung away. Iolo ducked, the little creature dipped past him then flew up to a shelf above the bed, where it came to rest.

Iolo straightened up. He saw a tiny bat clinging to something that lay on the very edge of the shelf. He cautiously extended his hand toward the bat, but the creature sensed movement; it wheeled away and this time headed straight for the open window. As it went, something toppled off the shelf and fell onto the pillow. It was a small wooden animal. *A horse, maybe,* Iolo thought, but without ears or tail, its mouth a jagged row of teeth, its eyes bulging and fierce.

He picked it up to replace it but found that it was looking at him and he couldn't do what he'd intended because the horse didn't want to be abandoned. It clung to his hand with an almost human insistence. So he put it in his pocket, took the binoculars, and left Gwyn's room.

❋ ❋ ❋

The others were already in the high field where Gwyn had first caught sight of the kite. And, as if to reward them, the great bird reappeared. They had no need of binoculars; it soared above them, an autumn bird, red-gold in the soft light, its tail spread in a wide triangle, the distinctive blaze of white on the underwings clearly visible. It swept down to the woods and they jumped on a stone wall to prolong the event.

"It lives here," Nia cried. "Right here, with us. Let's not tell anyone, ever. Let's keep it a secret, our bird!"

"Better warn Iolo it's a secret then," said Emlyn, nodding at a small figure bobbing up the track.

And Gwyn saw Iolo sprinting toward them, the binoculars

clutched in his hand. He waited until Iolo reached them before telling him the news. "Don't broadcast it, Iolo, we don't want strangers on our mountain."

"Looking for our kite," Nia added.

Iolo climbed up beside them, held the binoculars to his eyes and trained them onto the wood. But the kite didn't emerge. It had important business down there, behind the screen of colored leaves.

They sat on the wall and ate the apples that Emlyn's mother had provided and then they remembered Evan.

"He can't be lost," Gwyn said.

And Emlyn remarked, "My mom's taken a fancy to him, I bet."

It was intended as a joke, but for some reason, no one laughed because Evan Llŷr was the sort of person who might pose a threat to the most stable relationship. Gwyn knew this because Elinor Llewelyn's glance had excluded everyone but Evan; even Gwyn's own mother had recalled the soldier with a hint of something deeper than affection, and now cheeky, childish Nia had begun to watch this older man like a real, wide-eyed girl at last.

"Let's go," Gwyn said suddenly, "and find out where the major's gone."

They followed the stream down to Tŷ Bryn. It was a favorite route. They could leap over the water from side to side, onto dry islands of rock that rose clear of the sparkle and the spray.

Emlyn led the way with Nia close behind him, singing delightedly as she slipped and splashed through the water. Her voice was high and fluttery but she didn't care, the mountain always drew songs from her. Gwyn couldn't help laughing, and then he turned to see what had become of Iolo. The sky smoldered gold and scarlet where the sun had left it and he was about to remark on this when he noticed Iolo, unmoving, on his tiny island, staring at something in his hand.

"What've you got, Iolo?" Gwyn called. "Not a fish?" No, it was not a fish. He knew very well what it was. He could see the tiny label. He stepped into the stream, but he was shaking now and couldn't trust himself to move farther.

Iolo, looking up, said, "It's a horse, I think. I found it in your room and put it in my pocket. I didn't mean to keep it, honest!"

"Give it to me." He couldn't convey urgency, his words carried across the water in a dismal mutter.

"OK." Iolo raised his arm.

"No! Don't throw . . ." This time Gwyn found a scream, but it was too late. Distracted by Gwyn's cry, Iolo's aim went wild. The horse was free! It sailed over Gwyn's head and landed, with a soft splash, beyond him. The stream carried it away.

"Stop it!" Gwyn shrieked.

Nia looked back, still singing, and Emlyn shouted, "What's the matter?"

Gwyn couldn't explain; even if he had had the time, they wouldn't understand, and who could blame them. "Destroyer . . ." he mumbled. "Guard the prince . . . me . . . only me . . . dark . . ." Shaking, he tottered to the bank and crawled along the side of the stream crying, "Stop it! Stop it! *Please!*"

"Stop what?" Confused, Nia slithered into a deep pool and water gushed into her wellingtons.

"Horse," Gwyn moaned. "Black, very small." Willing strength into his knees, he got to his feet and ran past Nia, his eyes fixed on the water. "You wouldn't know," he gabbled feebly. "It's got no ears, no tail. Must stop it, see! Stop it! Stop it!"

"What's so special about it?" Emlyn peered into the stream.

"There isn't time," Gwyn mumbled breathlessly. "Help me, Emlyn. If you see it, keep it safe. It's a terrible thing." And he ran on helplessly, seeing nothing in the stream but weeds and pebbles.

"You'll never find it now," Emlyn called. "The current's too fast, and once it reaches the river . . ."

"I must!" Gwyn screeched and pelted on, now hopping sideways to scrutinize the water where it rippled over shallow pools, now trying to race the current. But he couldn't stop shaking; fear shattered his concentration. He knew the others were staring at him, bewildered and concerned. It was such a small thing. They must have thought he was crazy.

All at once the shaking stopped and Gwyn stood very still, reluctantly remembering who he was. Then, leaving the others without any explanation, he ran home.

He kicked his boots off in the porch and crashed through the kitchen door, provoking an angry, "Watch that door," from his mother scrubbing potatoes in the kitchen.

"Don't let anyone come upstairs, Mom," Gwyn cried.

"Whatever . . ." she began.

"I'm dead serious, Mom," he said.

The urgency in his voice must have impressed her because she said gently, "All right, *cariad*!"

He leaped up two flights of stairs, burst into his room, and taking a deep breath, sank onto his bed. He mustn't panic now. He could see a boy, himself, fearful and wide-eyed, staring out of a small oval mirror on the wall opposite. "Nothing ever comes quietly into your life, Gwyn Griffiths," he sadly told himself. "A soldier arrives and you know he's not what he seems. Then a mad prince decides on some devilishness, and you're the one to stop him, the only one. If it wasn't so tragic, I'd laugh," and he smiled ruefully at his troubled and too youthful reflection.

Something glistened in a dark recess. His spider was at work already. She had known what he needed even before he himself had become fully aware of it. He sat very still, watching a glossy cobweb begin to form. Like a tiny spark, Arianwen darted back and forth in a series of breathtaking acrobatics while her gossamer grew into a vast and glittering screen.

Gwyn got up and closed the curtains so that the luminous threads would reveal more clearly the landscape where he must work. There was no turning back. He couldn't dismiss the magic. He must trap the demon before it was too late.

The web was spattered with green and gold, like swathes of paint, changing hue in places, to form shadows and sunlit trees and hedges. Now autumn leaves fluttered below the green, and Gwyn could discern the lane where it twisted beyond Nain's cottage and descended to Tŷ Llŷr. And there, on the bend where the ground leveled out beside the stream, the chestnut tree surged up beside its neighbors, towering, like a huge pavilion hung with rosy-golden banners, and Gwyn saw what he had been hoping for: a dark figure stepping out of the stream — a crouching demon, hardly yet formed into a man, stealthy, believing himself free again. Gwyn held his breath and gathered his strength. He had to order his thoughts and take a chance with his power, even if it stunted him for another year — there was no other way.

The shadowy figure moved beneath the low branches of the chestnut tree and then emerged onto the lane. It was tall and straight now, more prince than demon. "You don't fool me," Gwyn muttered as his victim took three paces — One! Two! Three! — into the center, the very heart of Arianwen's web.

"*Daliwch ef!*" Gwyn cried. "Take him!"

And the tiny streak of silver flared toward the web's heart, covering in a shining blanket the image that trembled there. It took less than a minute.

"We have him!" Gwyn whispered triumphantly, and then from the shelf above Gwyn's bed, the silver pipe rocked and a cry issued from it, filling the room. The sadness of the sound overwhelmed Gwyn. His confidence ebbed and his clever victory all at once seemed meaningless. He had heard the captured demon howl before, but this voice was different. It was full of despair and a kind of submission.

Arianwen crept along a rafter and dropped onto his arm, as if in consolation.

The green-and-gold landscape began to dissolve. The shining threads slackened and drifted apart; colored strands floated to the ceiling and disintegrated. And the silver core dropped to the floor, a pile of glittering fragments. Gwyn knelt and touched them. Hard to believe that a moment ago they had formed the image of a man. He blew and the tiny particles melted into the dust of his room.

"What have we done, Arianwen?" Gwyn asked softly.

CHAPTER FOUR

Demon Prince

THE OTHER CHILDREN HAD REACHED TŶ BRYN. THEY STOOD by the gate not knowing whether to seek out their friend or leave him in peace. Emlyn and Nia understood Gwyn well enough to respect his sudden impulses, his request for solitude. But they had never seen him in such a violent state of agitation. It frightened Nia.

"Let's go and see the kittens again," Emlyn suggested. "We can wait in the barn till Gwyn is ready."

"I didn't mean to do anything wrong," Iolo said for the tenth time. "It was only an old piece of wood. How can it be valuable?"

"It'll turn up," Emlyn reassured him. "Come on, we'll go and find out what it's all about." He turned in through the gate and walked up the path, with Iolo hopping nervously after him.

Nia held back; she noticed that Gwyn's curtains were drawn. Something was happening in his attic room. It must be dark in there. It reminded her of sickness and unnatural sleep. She walked away from the house calling, "I'll see you later."

She had just turned the last bend before the lane made its

steep descent to Emlyn's home when she saw someone climbing out of the stream behind the chestnut tree. *Evan must have been wandering there,* she thought. Perhaps he had found Gwyn's horse.

Yes, it was Evan; he was tall and had to stoop beneath the branches. He stepped into the lane, took three paces toward her and lifted his hand to wave, then he fell — and went on falling!

Nia found herself running. The prince had made no sound when he slipped to the ground but Nia sensed a cry so terrible it seemed as though her own breath was caught in it. She saw a man lying motionless, but she could still feel him falling, falling, falling, and could hear his descending sigh, while all about him was utterly silent, utterly still.

When she reached Evan he had turned onto his back. He was lying among the broken chestnut shells, his arms spread wide, his fingers buried in dead leaves. He smiled at Nia and said, "Don't be frightened. No bones broken!"

Then he sat up and brushed himself free of dust and dead leaves, while Nia watched, speechless. But when he eventually got to his feet, she flung her arms around his waist and buried her face in the rough wool of his sweater. "I thought you had died," she murmured.

Evan laughed and said, "I am very much alive!"

She felt the laugh deep inside his body and a pulse racing through him, angry and irregular, as though it had just been awakened. His arms around her shoulders were hot and heavy, but he was shivering.

They walked up the lane to get Iolo for the journey home,

Evan keeping Nia's hand in his own and gradually his shivering subsided.

I will protect him, Nia thought. *He is my prince and in danger, but I shall save him, somehow.* From whom or what she should save him she didn't know. Nor did she know that she was too late!

Gwyn's curtains were still drawn when they reached Tŷ Bryn, and Nia was reluctant to go in, so she called to Iolo from the gate, and heard a muffled pleading for "Just one minute longer with the kittens, *please!*" and then Gwyn's mother saw Evan from the window and ran to open the kitchen door.

"Come and have a cup of tea while you wait," she suggested. "It's Evan Llŷr, isn't it?"

"It is, and your sister, Elinor, has already entertained me," the soldier told her.

"I see," Glenys Griffiths looked disappointed. "Did she give you cake, too? Elinor doesn't like baking. I've got fresh fruit-cake here!"

"I can't resist," said Evan Llŷr.

Glenys's smile seemed to indicate more than ordinary pleasure; in fact, Nia had rarely seen Gwyn's mother so animated, but Mr. Griffiths came through the yard just then, and his wife's expression stiffened into awkward uncertainty. "You remember Evan Llŷr, Ivor, don't you? He used to help the Lloyds with the lambing."

"I don't remember," Mr. Griffiths muttered.

"Of course you do." Glenys pulled at her apron nervously.

"I said I don't," said Ivor Griffiths. He did not welcome visitors but on this occasion his hostility seemed personal.

The soldier, however, seemed unperturbed. "It's been ten years," he said, "and people can't be expected to remember."

"Evan's staying for a bit," Glenys said boldly. "Are you coming in then, Ivor?"

Ivor stood rooted to his earth. "What is this, a party? It's milking time. Where's Gwyn?"

Gwyn's father can be so savage, Nia thought. "I'll go get him, if you like," Nia said.

"Well, he's . . . busy, Nia," Mrs. Griffiths began.

"Tell him it's five minutes or there'll be no pocket money," her husband growled.

"Yes, and I'll knock," Nia told Gwyn's mother.

As she left them, she heard Evan say, "I'll help with the cows, Ivor, I haven't forgotten how." But Nia did not hear the reply.

She knocked on Gwyn's door, as she had promised, but receiving no answer, went in. Gwyn's room was dim and airless. It seemed to be full of some kind of dust: particles of gossamer drifted just beneath the rafters and tiny, broken threads sparkled in the gloomy recesses under the beams. So Gwyn was back at work. She knew how reluctant he was. What had forced his hand at last?

Gwyn was sitting on the bed with his strange silver spider nestling in his hand. "I know it's milking time," he said.

"Are you all right?" she asked. "Did you find it, that horse?"

"In a way," he replied, and then he looked sideways at her and mumbled, "I had to use the power, though."

He hadn't mentioned his power for a long time. He used to call it magic, but considered himself too old for that word now.

"What did you do?" she sat beside him.

"It was Arianwen," he said. "She showed me where he was and we caught him, she and I, we wrapped him up. Trapped him!"

"How?" she asked gently.

"In the web. I saw him under the chestnut tree. He'd escaped you see, from the horse."

"Who escaped? What was it in the horse?" Nia asked, alarmed by the unnatural glitter in his dark eyes.

"A demon," Gwyn said.

She thought of the cry that had taken her breath away and her prince lying among the broken chestnut shells. "Evan fell under the chestnut tree," she said. "I thought he had died!"

They regarded each other, trying to relate what she had said to a captured demon. And it seemed to Nia that Gwyn suddenly reached a conclusion he might have been afraid to share with her. Then he shook his head and said, "Perhaps I'd better remind you of a story."

Nia might have warned him of his father's threat then, but Evan would help with the cows, and Emlyn, probably. She had to know this story. "Remind me, then," she urged.

"Remember the presents Nain gave me for my ninth birthday?" Gwyn said. "The seaweed that brought a ship from outer space, and the scarf that called my lost sister back for a while."

Nia nodded. She had been the only one to share Gwyn's secret and it was not so long ago that the extraordinary ship had returned and nearly taken Emlyn away forever. It was only Gwyn's power that had saved his cousin. A little sadness always seemed to linger about Gwyn, however, because he had been unable to keep his sister with him. But Nia felt that, in many ways, the lost girl was still there, on the mountain. Mrs. Griffiths kept her daughter's room just as she had left it — with rose petals in the drawers, dresses hanging in the closet, and dolls displayed on the dressing table, as though any day Bethan might walk through the door with a bouquet of flowers she had wandered off to find. It was Nia who had chosen Bethan's name for her new baby sister, two years ago.

"And there was the brooch," Gwyn went on, "that became Arianwen when I gave it to the wind.

"The broken horse was another gift," Gwyn said, and then he grunted, "Some gift! I wouldn't be telling you this if I didn't think you'd understand, Nia. But I believe you're the only one who can believe in the impossible. Am I right?"

Honored by this description of herself, she eagerly agreed, "You are!"

"The horse was given to my grandmother by her great-great-grandmother, who was a witch," he glanced at her, "if you can believe that."

"I can," she said.

"I must keep it safe, she told me, never let it go. For I was the guardian, the magician who had inherited the power of Gwydion. But even Nain didn't know what that horse contained."

"And did you find out?" Nia asked.

He avoided a direct answer. "I had to search the legends," he said, and from beneath his pillow, took a book already open at a page that had evidently been more than just slept on, because it was stained with thumb marks and wrinkled with damp breath.

"They say this story is more than two thousand years old," Gwyn went on. "For hundreds of years, bards and storytellers kept it alive until it was written down, maybe hundreds of years later. Shall I read it?"

"Yes please," Nia said fervently. Gwyn was the best story-teller she knew, describing events with such passionate meaning that heroes and heroines seemed to leap before her, drawing armies and castles behind them, in a dazzling atmosphere that quite excluded all her immediate surroundings.

Gwyn cleared his throat in a rather theatrical way and began, "'Long, long ago, when Britain was a land of wild forests, Bendigeidfran, the Blessed Bran, son of Llŷr, was king. He was a mighty man, a giant. Men thought him a god. He had a brother, Manawydan, and a sister, Branwen . . .'"

"The fairest maiden in all Britain," Nia said, happy to demonstrate her knowledge.

"D'you know it all, then?" Gwyn asked tersely.

"No, no! That's all I can remember. Please go on," Nia begged.

"The next part is what matters," Gwyn told her. "Will you promise to keep quiet?"

She nodded, obediently mute.

"'Bendigeidfran had two half brothers, sons of his mother, Penarddun. Nisien was a kind and peaceful man; Efnisien, his brother, was the very opposite. Wherever there was peace, Efnisien would cause strife!

"'On a sparkling summer day, Bendigeidfran was sitting with his nobles on a rock at Harlech when he saw a most wonderful fleet sail into the bay. One ship outstripped the others: bright banners waved, its prow was painted gold and it flew a flag of brocaded silk. Even from afar it glittered like a wonderful toy, but for all its joyful color, its promise of good tidings, it brought nothing but future sadness. It carried Matholwch, King of Ireland, who had come to ask for Princess Branwen to be his wife.

"'And it was agreed that Branwen should marry Matholwch. But when Efnisien discovered this he was consumed with rage. "My sister shall not marry Matholwch," he ranted. "A maiden so excellent she belongs in Britain and married to a British prince".'"

"D'you think he loved her?" Nia asked, forgetting her promise.

Gwyn frowned severely and continued, "'And he maimed the Irish king's horses: He cut off their lips, their ears, their tails, and even their eyelids until they screamed and no one could lay a hand on them. And because of this and the shame Bendigeidfran felt on Efnisien's behalf, he gave to Matholwch Britain's most precious possession — the great cauldron of rebirth wherein a dead man could be born again. Matholwch took the gift but he was still not appeased, and once in his own country, he treated his new wife, Branwen, in a terrible fashion. He banished her to the kitchens where she was beaten every day and although she bore Matholwch a son, still he would not honor her. In her lonely cell, Branwen found a starling and trained it to seek out her brothers, telling them of her misery. As soon as he received word of her plight, King Bendigeidfran and his brothers crossed the Irish Sea with their army. The Irish were mortally afraid, for Bendigeidfran strode waist-high across the sea. They did not want to do battle with such a man and they hastily built a mighty house to honor him, for he was of too great a stature for any of their buildings.

"'But the wily Irish did not intend to let the British live. Inside the great house they hung two hundred bags of hide, and in every bag hid an Irish soldier, and that night every Briton would have died were it not for Efnisien, who was their greatest warrior in strategy and courage. It was he who first entered the house to ensure King Bendigeidfran's safety.

"'"What is in those bags?" Efnisien asked the Irish.

"'"Flour," they answered.

"'Efnisien approached the first bag — he touched it suspiciously and knew it to be a soldier. With his great hands he ruthlessly crushed the skull he felt inside the bag. And this he did with every one until he had killed all the soldiers hidden there, and the Irish, being too ashamed to admit their treachery, could do nothing to stop him.

"'And that night a feast was held in the house and it was agreed that Gwern, the son of Branwen and Matholwch, should be heir to both the kings thus uniting their countries. But all of a sudden, Efnisien rose up wrathfully and cast the boy into the fire, and it was done so fast that no one could stop the deed.'"

Nia knew now why she had tried to forget the story. She wanted to ask if it was insanity or hate or terrible love that had caused Efnisien's dreadful act, but she realized that in the passing of time and the route from bard to bard, the meaning and the cause had become blurred and then forgotten. "Go on," she whispered.

Gwyn looked at her over the top of the book and continued without looking at it. It was obvious that he knew the next part by heart.

"'And then there was a tumult in the house as the Irish and the British took up arms against one another. And when the Irish saw that they might be defeated, they began to kindle the cauldron of rebirth so that their army would be reborn. Efnisien, seeing that his soldiers had no hope against a ghostly army, cried, "Woe is me that I should cause the death of the men of Britain, and shame on me if I do not seek their deliverance!" And he lay down among the Irish dead and, believing him to be an Irish corpse, they threw him into the boiling cauldron, a living man. And he stretched himself out in the cauldron and burst it into four pieces, and his heart burst also!'"

Gwyn looked into the book again but did not continue the story. He had told Nia all she needed to know. The sadness increased on every further page, for in the end she remembered, Branwen and the king died, too.

"We are Llŷrs, of course," Nia said thoughtfully, "through our mother, though I can't believe we're related to a legend in any way."

"I seem to be," Gwyn said wryly.

Should one be consoled for being a magician? Nia wondered, but asked instead, "You think it is the spirit of Efnisien then, trapped in that horse?"

"Yes! I do believe it is!"

"And when Iolo lost him in the stream, he was free for a while."

"For a while, but I caught him, didn't I?" he attempted a reassuring grin. "Before he could do any harm."

"Then where is he now?"

Gwyn shrugged. "I don't know, Nia! I made a spell and it went astray somehow. I don't know why. Don't worry, I'll find the horse. Right now I'd better get downstairs or I'll be late for milking!"

But the cows were already in the barn, and Mr. Griffiths, in a better mood now, was chatting to Evan in the yard. Evan seemed reluctant to leave the mountain. "You keep the sun so long up here," he told the farmer.

When they went home, at last, the sky was a riot of violent colors, and a lonely bird, hidden in the chestnut tree, cried out, like an omen.

❊ ❊ ❊

They soon became used to having a soldier at number six. His was an easy presence, quiet, unobtrusive. He took his breakfast early and was out of the house before the morning scramble: the banging on the bathroom door, shouts for more milk, more toast, the noisy hunt for combs, clean socks, sandwiches, and schoolbooks. There was seldom a time when all eight children had everything they needed, never a time when one hadn't had to run to catch up with the rest.

Evan Llŷr caused quite a stir in Pendewi, though.

"Related, is he?" Mrs. Bowen, who owned the yarn shop, asked Betty Lloyd, who had taken Nia to choose colors for a new cardigan.

"My cousin," Betty smiled possessively.

"Dashing, isn't he?"

"Well, I wouldn't . . ." She was proud of Evan but had never been one to boast. "Yes, he is good-looking, isn't he?" she coyly conceded.

"And a major, too, I hear!"

"That's right. Nia, come closer, *cariad*. Nia's good with colors. I never choose without her now."

"Been in the army long, has he?" Mrs. Bowen resumed her ferreting.

"Fifteen years or more."

"Is he on leave?"

"That's it. Sick leave!"

"Was he wounded?"

"That's it! In Belfast!"

"Whereabouts?" Mrs. Bowen leaned closer, eager for details that might have to be confided in a whisper because of Nia.

"Whereabouts? Oh, well . . . I didn't ask." Mrs. Lloyd stepped away from Mrs. Bowen's prying black eyes.

Nia shuffled inside the door. She hated the way Mrs. Bowen probed for every detail. Dissecting her prince like a specimen, caught under the glass, going on about his wounds. Why wouldn't they leave him alone? The twins were just as bad. As soon as Evan returned from wherever he fled in his dark car they would start, "What happened, Evan? Was it a bomb, Evan?"

"Was it a bomb?" Mrs. Bowen nosed for the scent. "Belfast, you said. Bound to have been a bomb!"

"Well, it's difficult, Joan." Betty was flustered. She didn't know, that was the truth. No one knew, for sure, what Evan's trouble had been. Questions often flickered on her tongue but were always left unspoken. She feared they might drive her Evan away. He had never volunteered information.

"Lucky his face wasn't scarred or we wouldn't be so interested, would we?" Mrs. Bowen giggled. "Are you with me?"

"Yes." Mrs. Lloyd shuffled the skeins of yarn. "Nia, come here and look at this pink."

Nia, gazing through the window, had seen a black car gliding smooth and quiet down the High Street. Evan was home early today. Where did he go, she wondered, every day? Out all day and at night restless — moving around in the room beneath hers. She would lie awake holding her breath, taut with curiosity, listening for every small sound: a step, a creak, a cough, a sigh. Her prince was so near and yet so completely mysterious.

"Nia," Mrs. Lloyd called impatiently.

The black car pulled up outside number six. Nia rushed to the counter. "That one's too pale, and those are too bright," she said, pushing the skeins of yarn back across the counter. "And that one's really horrible, like plastic flowers."

"Flamingo is a very popular color," Mrs. Bowen bristled.

"I'd go for green, Mom," Nia said.

"But, Nia, we agreed on pink, I thought, to go with Bethan's dress." Betty Lloyd rubbed her forehead.

"I give up then." Nia made a dash for the door.

"Green, is it?" Mrs. Bowen sighed dramatically and bent under the counter.

Mrs. Lloyd, confused, muttered. "I'm not sure, Nia . . . ?" She turned to her daughter.

"I've got piles of homework, Mom," Nia said. "And green will do," and she slipped through the door leaving it open so that the shop bell rang continuously at the back of the building, where Mrs. Bowen's mother made baby clothes and never answered the door anyway.

She heard her mother shout as she sped away, but she didn't try to decipher the message. She was afraid Catrin would be playing hostess. She was right. When she ran into the house, Evan was stepping through the kitchen door and Catrin was already pouring tea for him.

"You're early today," Nia said boldly. "Where've you been?"

"Nowhere and everywhere," Evan replied.

"Is that a riddle?"

"It could be, but it's not. I've been in the mountains. I climbed, sat and watched clouds, went to sleep!"

"Were you tired?" Nia thought of the nightly creaks and sighs.

"Shut up, Nia," Catrin snapped. "Leave Evan alone."

It wasn't like Catrin to be harsh. Stung, Nia decided to tease her sister. "Had a bad day, then? Didn't Michael say 'hello!'?"

"Don't be ridiculous!" The tea that Catrin was pouring would have overflowed the cup, if Evan had not put out a hand to steady her. He gently removed the teapot and set it on the table. Then he held Catrin's hand in both of his, and looking from one sister to the other, said quietly, "Let's not have quarreling in the kitchen."

Nia burned with unspoken sentences. The sight of those clasped hands troubled her. Perhaps something of her worry conveyed itself to Evan for he released Catrin and said, "You've asked me questions, Nia, now tell me about your day."

She sat beside him on the bench, not too close, but near enough to notice a tiny fleck of red in his black hair, just behind the ear. "I've been to school," she said. "There's nothing interesting about that, is there?"

Evan laughed and it was such a carefree sound that the girls laughed with him, and gradually the tension that had filled the cramped little kitchen was diffused and they even noticed that the evening sun, slanting into the room, was bouncing reflections from the silverware on the table, up to the low ceiling. Evan took a spoon, and twisting it through the air, made light dance over Catrin's golden hair, and then on Nia's dark braids. So both the girls had to take silverware, Nia a teaspoon and Catrin a knife, and turn the lights on Evan, over his face and around his head, like a glittering crown. And Nia noticed yet another streak of red in the black hair, and then another.

"We're going swimming!" The twins were in the doorway, watching the show.

"D'you want to come?" Siôn addressed himself to Evan.

"No, it's too cold," Evan said.

"It's not, it's great, warmer than summer!" Enthusiasm always made Gareth yell.

"All the same, I'd rather not." The soldier drummed his fingers on the table.

"We go down by the bridge, it's not deep, but you can swim a bit," Siôn persisted.

"Evan's busy," Catrin interceded. "Go on, twins, we'll come later."

Siôn would have gone then, but Gareth was always one to push even when the cause seemed hopeless. "Is it your scars?" he asked hopefully. "We don't care. Are there scars where you were wounded? I'd be proud if I had scars!" He edged closer to the table trying to fathom his unsoldierly cousin, completely unprepared for the onslaught he provoked.

Violence sliced through the air as Evan leaped to his feet and thundered, "There are no wounds! No scars! Nothing, understand? Nothing . . . nothing . . . nothing!" He towered above them, his fine face distorted with fury, and Nia felt the room shudder at the outrage that poured into it. A monstrous stranger glowered there, not Evan, and to her horror she saw tears on his face, as though he despaired of the wrath that had shaken through him.

Instinctively she covered her eyes and heard the boys shuffle away, frightened into silence. The emptiness that followed their retreat was all the more alarming after such an outburst.

When she dared to risk a furtive glance into the room she found the prince sitting beside her, looking pale and all used up, as though he was bewildered by the anger, and wondering who he was.

Catrin's voice broke into the stillness, saying shakily, "Let's go and watch the boys, right, Nia?"

Nia nodded, still too nervous to speak, and to their surprise Evan said, very slowly, "I'll come with you."

And then they heard Bethan crying from the room above.

"Bethan!" Catrin cried. "I forgot her. I told Mom I'd look after her."

She ran out of the kitchen and was about to mount the stairs when Mrs. Lloyd came through the front door, flustered from her interview in the wool shop and calling, "Nia, why did you run off? Mrs. Bowen persuaded me to get flamingo pink and now . . . I don't know . . . Are you going out again?"

Nia and Evan had come to meet her in the hall, and Evan said quietly, "We're going to watch the twins in the river."

"But Bethan's crying, Mom," Catrin told her.

"I'll see to her. You go on!" Mrs. Lloyd ushered them out awkwardly. She wanted a little peace before her husband came in from the shop. She wanted to think about flamingo pink wool and what to cook for supper. "No hurry," she called after them and added, "You'll be staying in tonight then, Evan?"

He turned back, confused again it seemed, and said, "Yes, I'll be with you."

❋ ❋ ❋

The weather was still extraordinary. There had hardly been a breeze since the storm that had preceded Evan's arrival. Every day after school, boys would migrate to the river, trying to prolong the sensation of a never-ending summer. And the evening mist would close about them, settling softly into the brittle bronze fields, a warm mist, scented with ripening fruit.

The girls wandered up High Street with Evan between them, and Nia was aware of fluttering lace curtains and glances across the street. Middle-aged mothers smiled at Evan over their bundles of late shopping, and Catrin's friends stared, openly envious, while the boys — suspicious and ill at ease — pretended disinterest, but watched their progress all the way to the bridge.

"Anyone would think you were an alien," Nia whispered to Evan.

And he bent down and said, very seriously, "Perhaps I am!"

No, Nia thought, *you are not from Out There, and neither are you from Here.* She began to think of the gods and princes who inhabited the Celtic Otherworld, sometimes leaping out to breathe real mountain air before slipping back into their misty legends. "Perhaps you're from the Otherworld," she murmured.

Evan heard her and asked, "Do you believe in pagan gods then, Nia?"

"I don't know," she truthfully replied.

Catrin, puzzled, inquired, "Are you two playing a game?"

"It could be a game," Evan mused.

They had reached the bridge and looked down on the four boys in the river. Alun and Iolo waved when they saw Evan, but the twins ignored their audience, they splashed and shouted at each other still unable to bring themselves to look at their cousin after his stormy outburst.

"Let's see, now, do you know your legends, Catrin?" Evan pursued the matter of gods.

Catrin struggled. "Nia's the expert," she said.

"Don't tell me you've forsaken words for music!" Evan's tone was light and teasing, but Catrin would not answer. She had seen a horse and rider approaching down the hill.

So Evan stroked her hair over and over, while he gently reminded her of the stories she seemed to have forgotten. And, as the horseman drew nearer, he put his arm about her shoulder and his mouth close to her hair and whispered something that made her turn from Michael McGoohan and look at Evan with astonishment and, it seemed to Nia, recognition.

All at once, Nia felt isolated. She ran to the end of the bridge and began to shout encouragement at the boys, trying to stifle the bewildering ache she felt at the sight of those two heads, black and gold, so close. But she never took her eyes off the horseman. She saw him reach the figures on the bridge, saw Evan turn slowly, still keeping Catrin close, and look up at the rider.

And then there was a scream. It was the horse. Something must have startled him. The sound he made was awful and full of pain. He reared up, his front hooves cleaving the air, while Michael clung to his back, terrified, shouting angry oaths at the man and the girl.

He was usually such a quiet horse, big and gentle. Nia knew him well, they all knew him. His name was Glory.

Michael almost had the horse under control when Glory began to cavort about on the bridge. Catrin called out helplessly, "What did I do?" but Evan stood watching, very calm, and did nothing. Then Michael began to use his whip, a thing he rarely did; he pulled at the bit and Glory screamed again, then the horse charged, straight at Nia.

She crouched against the wall and the great animal thundered past, close enough for her to smell his terrible fear and to feel the thud of Michael's helpless body on the saddle, and then Glory had left the bridge and was hurtling down the bank.

Nia leaped up and followed, perhaps believing that by doing this she could help in some way. But the horse plunged into the water and began stumbling and rearing across the river, while sheets of spray burst over him. The terrified swimmers floundered out of his way and Michael cried, "Glory! Glory, boy!" as his boots skimmed the water.

Black Glory careered toward the far side of the river, and as he trampled the rushes, a bird soared out, shrieking. The horse screamed in panic, vaulted onto the bank, and sped over the yellow fields, slipping through the close air as though he was haunted.

When Nia turned back, the mist was settling and she could hardly make out the figures on the bridge. Even as she watched, Evan and Catrin began to leave her; they became as insubstantial as ghosts, receding into a world of their own where she couldn't follow.

She ran home, superstitiously urging herself out of the misty ring of enchantment where there was no special place for her. The sound of Bethan's crying was almost reassuring until she remembered that her little sister rarely cried and had never been inconsolable.

When Nia tumbled into the kitchen, Bethan glared sullenly

from her mother's lap. Her tearstained face was crumpled with exhaustion.

"What is it, Nia?" Mrs. Lloyd asked, alarmed at Nia's sudden arrival, afraid that a boy was drowned or hurt at the very least.

"I didn't — like it there, Mom," Nia said, fumbling for a description of events. "Michael's horse — he's ill or something!"

"No one's hurt?" Mrs. Lloyd stroked the distressed child's head.

"No, Mom!" *Only me,* she could have said. *Because they've shut me out, those two on the bridge, and something is happening that I don't want to understand.*

Bethan began to sob again and Nia asked, "What's the matter with Bethie? She's been crying for ages. It's not like her!"

"Oh, Nia, I don't know!" She gave a familiar hard-pressed mother's sigh. "I found Iolo's toys all broken on the landing. He shouldn't have left them there, but all the same, they could have brushed them aside, whoever it was, not stamped on them in such a way."

"Was Bethan there?" Nia inquired. The little girl had broken precious things before, in an accidental baby way.

"She was in Catrin's room," said Mrs. Lloyd indignantly. "Besides her tiny fingers couldn't have done — that!"

The damage was worse than usual it seemed. Nia went to inspect.

Iolo's farm animals lay scattered on the dark uncarpeted floorboards. At first glance they seemed to have been kicked around or trampled underfoot by someone carelessly hastening toward the stairs. But when Nia knelt to gather them up she found herself touching severed limbs and tails, twisted heads, and tiny slivers of metal. The boys had never destroyed one another's toys with such deadly purpose, and only the horses, Iolo's favorites, had been broken: shire horses, hunters, tiny Shetland ponies, even a mare and her foal had been damaged almost beyond recognition, while the other animals, and even a farmer and his milkmaid, still stood, unharmed, beside the wall.

She dropped the small sad pieces into her pocket, wondering how she would break the news to Iolo. What had possessed the person who had done such a cruel thing? She couldn't believe that it was someone she knew, one of the family.

Outside the mist intensified and a purple dusk invaded the house, ironing shadows out of corners and spreading them thickly through the rooms. Bethan began to wail again and the thin, hunted sound made Nia shiver. Bethan had been a witness. She knew who had destroyed the toy horses, but could not speak his name.

CHAPTER FIVE

Horses

GWYN'S FRENCH BOOK FLUTTERED OUT OF REACH. THE SCHOOL bus waited halfway up a high and windy hill in Pendewi where anything light and unguarded was at risk. Gwyn had no liking for French but he hadn't thought the wind would take him literally when he had wished aloud that he'd never have to see or hear a foreign verb again. But he'd packed his backpack carelessly after the last class; a potato chip bag had flown out, and as he'd bent to catch it, the backpack had flapped open, leaving his homework at the mercy of the wind.

As he crawled along the path, grabbing at his drifting papers, he saw Nia running up to him. She should have been going in the opposite direction. The Lloyds didn't need a bus; they lived ten minutes away from the school.

Nia caught the escaping French book, stifled its flapping, and thrust it under her arm, crying, "Gwyn, can you come home with me?"

"I've got homework," Gwyn said halfheartedly. It wasn't that he was unhappy to see Nia, but it was embarrassing to have a girl stop you under the eyes of a busful of children; they were already laughing at him. He knelt on the path, stuffing pens and papers back into his backpack.

The bus drove up to him, its door invitingly open, giving him a chance at least. "Are you getting on or not, boy?" Mr. Roberts, the driver, looked down at him. "Or is it the girlfriend, tonight?" He was always joking at other people's expense.

"Please, Gwyn?" Nia stood panting beside him. She held out the French book.

"Look, I've got to . . ." Gwyn glanced helplessly at the bus.

"Well, boy!" Mr. Roberts said.

"Please!" Nia begged.

Mr. Roberts, star of Pendewi Amateur Dramatic Society, sighed theatrically. "I can see I'm not wanted," he shouted back into the bus and was rewarded with giggles and donkey brays.

It was now impossible for Gwyn to get on the bus. The door slammed shut, but as the vehicle drove away, Gwyn saw Emlyn peering from the back window. One sympathetic face made up for all the rest.

"Tell Mom I'll be late!" Gwyn mouthed at his cousin.

Emlyn nodded and the bus vanished over the lip of the hill.

"Gee, Nia!" Gwyn said angrily. "Couldn't it have waited?"

"No," she said, and he became aware that she was anxious and lost, like someone clinging to a hope, and he was it.

"OK." He grinned amiably. "Thanks for saving the book."

"I don't want to go straight home," she said.

"I'm not staying up here, at least let's go down the hill a bit." He pulled the hood of his jacket over his eyes, squeezing a smile out of her at last. Things were easier then.

They sat on the stone wall that curved around the base of the school hill. It was an ancient wall, patched and rebuilt over the years, reinforced with concrete and thickened with sand-colored rocks so that, where the stark gray stones remained, it seemed as though the wall had been blasted by thunderbolts. No one knew its beginnings. Perhaps if it were not there, hill and school would have tumbled into the river.

"I've told Alun to tell Mom I'm at Gwyneth's," Nia began, "so there's no hurry."

"Nia, why did you lie?" Gwyn groaned. "There was no need."

"It's a habit," she replied, kicking the wall, "and it's easier." .

"It's a bad habit," he remarked, "and in the end it makes things worse, you know that. You're so crazy sometimes."

He realized he was going to have to pay for that remark. She would keep him up here for another half hour before coming to the point if he didn't watch out. "Come on." He nudged her encouragingly.

"It's difficult." She looked at her dangling feet. "A horrible thing happened yesterday. We were all there but we can't talk about it; everyone's pretending they didn't see it, even the boys. So I have to tell you because you're outside it all and can tell me if it matters or if I'm silly about a . . . a crazed horse."

"Horse?" It was the word that made him shiver, not the cold.

"Glory!" Nia said.

"Glory?" Gwyn had no liking for the McGoohans, show-offs all of them, but Glory was not a McGoohan — he was a beautiful creature, you couldn't help admiring him. "What about Glory?" he asked.

"We were on the bridge," Nia went on. "Catrin, Evan, and me, watching the boys in the river. And Michael rode up on Glory. He always puts on an act, you know. He takes off his hat and sweeps it through the air, and then he bows to Catrin as if she's a princess."

"I know, I know," Gwyn said hastily. He'd seen Michael's little show and thought he looked like a fool stuck up on his big horse, acting like a lord. If only he knew how Pendewi boys laughed. And Catrin was so taken with it; Gwyn hated that.

"Sometimes he lifts Catrin onto Glory's back," Nia continued. "They don't go anywhere. Just sit there whispering, and she should be practicing you know, for her grade eight music."

Gwyn began to wonder how many details he would have to listen to before Nia got to the point and then she said, "But yesterday it all went wrong," and he realized that she was still so frightened by what she had seen that she didn't know how to describe it.

"Go on." He hoped he sounded sympathetic. He was eager for more, and sorry for the way he had begun the discussion.

"Like I said, we were on the bridge, and Michael rode up but when Glory saw us, he screamed, and then he ran as if . . . he had seen a ghost. There was nothing else, you see, no frightening sounds, nothing to startle him, and he's such a quiet horse, even in traffic. He never, never panics."

"Who was he looking at, Nia?" Gwyn peered into her troubled face.

"It wasn't me," she replied, "because I was farther away, and I don't think it was Catrin."

She was so distressed she couldn't bring herself to name the man. Images moved in Gwyn's mind, sensations, just out of reach: the telephone, the soldier by the water and the bleak touch of his hand, the howl dredged out of the past when the spider had caught her prey. And Nia knew what was on his mind, she had been with him at every step because she said in a surprised tone, "He was hurt when he fell, more than we know. Part of him called out so sadly but" — she screwed up her face so that every feature frowned at Gwyn — "he didn't make a sound."

"And you don't make sense," Gwyn said, trying to cheer her up. They had been tossing the soldier between them, now it was time to name him. "So Evan Llŷr frightened a horse; Evan Llŷr fell and did some silent crying!" He tried to sound matter-of-fact because he was going to need her help and she must remain calm. "Evan Llŷr is a strange man," he said. "What's his past? Who is he? Do we know he is your cousin for sure?"

Her reply to these questions was not what he expected. A rosy tint began to liven up her pale face and she looked away from him as she murmured, "I've been thinking he was a prince or something, you know, like in the stories, 'Sleeping Beauty' and 'Cinderella.'"

"Aw, come off it!" He jumped down from the wall.

"The frog prince," she said desperately, "or Rapunzel's poor blind prince . . . or . . ."

"Let's walk a bit," he said.

But she remained where she was, high on her ancient wall, demanding his attention and what had begun as a silly list that he had been eager to dismiss, gradually evolved into a sort of index that could, if he chose the right name, lead him to the core of his search, for she began to name the heroes of Wales.

"Prince Pwyll," she cried, leaping to her feet and running along the wall, "or brave Culwch and the giant's daughter, or," she gazed over the town to where the mountains unfolded in waves of fading blue, as though the hero she sought still slept there, waiting for her cry of recognition, "or maybe a king," she said. "Arthur or Bran."

Why didn't she mention that other prince? Was she too frightened even to think of him? After all, Gwyn admitted to himself, there was still no proof. "Not Bran," he muttered, but he kept the rest of his information locked inside his head where it could hurt no one but himself. It hissed and made him feel sick and dizzy, and he longed to shout, "Efnisien, prince of madness and the dark," but instead he began to run into the wind hoping his fears would be blown away.

"Don't go." Nia leaped down and ran after him. "I haven't told you all of it."

"Well, what then?" He stopped and waited, almost dreading the rest of her story.

"When I got home," she said, "I found Iolo's toy horses on the landing. They'd all been broken in terrible ways, twisted, flat, stomped on, and," she hesitated, "their tails and heads had been torn off, and Bethan was crying and crying, but it can't have been her, she's too small."

No, *not Bethan*, Gwyn thought, *but perhaps she had been there, watching, while someone stormed past her, overcome by a two-thousand-year-old rage.*

"No one knows who did it," Nia went on, "but we're all watching one another, wondering, and there's a horrible feeling in the house. And I thought of you and your horse. You said if you didn't find it something terrible would happen. Well, where is it?"

"I've been wondering myself," he said miserably. "I was so sure I had trapped that crazed spirit, even though I couldn't find the horse. But something's wrong. I've been careless."

She tapped his arm and asked, "What have you done?"

"It's what I haven't done," he sighed. "I have a foreboding, but I can't tell you yet what it's about."

"Can I help?"

"Yes! Keep an eye out for that horse I lost. I believe you might find it. I didn't describe it, but I will now. It has no ears, no tail; its lips are gone, its eyelids are cut away, so the eyes are always afraid, and the mouth is always screaming."

She stood away from him, screwing her face up again; it was a habit she had but anyone would have done the same.

"And there's a label around its neck," he went on. "It says '*Dim hon!* Not this!' Because it must never be used, never left unguarded where its spirit can escape."

"But it has escaped, hasn't it?" she accused him. "Because all that stuff about your spider catching it just wasn't true, was it? Was it?" And she jabbed nervously at him.

"Look," he tried to sound confident. "I may not like what I

am, but Arianwen and I, well, it's no use denying it, we can make things happen, and yes, we did stop that spirit. If we hadn't, there would have been a storm, don't you see? There would have been hail and thunder, things would have died. As far as I know, he's a little pile of dust, it's just . . ."

"Just . . . ?" she echoed.

"Just that I don't like losing things." His halfhearted laugh suddenly became real because she looked so funny, her small scowling face twisting around like a puzzled bird. "Let's go to your house now, and perhaps your mother will give me some tea before we have to figure out who's picking me up or who's taking me home."

"Evan might take you." She smiled. "And give me a ride, too."

He did not want to consider her suggestion. "I could always fly," he said and then, in an attempt to keep the conversation lighthearted, he added, "I don't see why ski lifts are reserved for Switzerland."

Nia giggled aloud and they ran, still laughing, around the curve of the hill and on down into Pendewi, only to discover that they were about to take part in a curious drama.

There were three people outside number six, obstructing the passage of the butcher's customers. Michael McGoohan, a pedestrian today, was hopping on and off the curb like an angry wasp in his tweed jacket and yellow corduroys. He was shouting at Catrin so that people turned to stare at her, while she stood with her back to the wall, her arms folded, head down, and golden hair hiding her face. Michael seemed small without his horse, a wispy man with faded curls, but perhaps he looked that way because Evan Llŷr was there beside Catrin, his dark presence holding the focus like a magnet, so that all about him seemed incidental: unnecessary paraphernalia that hovered beneath him like so many insects.

"Poor Michael," Gwyn murmured without compassion.

They gathered speed and then came to a halt simultaneously, as though each knew what the other felt, for they had come within the circle of the extraordinary scene and were not part of it.

"You'll have to!" Michael cried in his sweet Irish tenor. "Come with me now and see for yourself."

"I don't want to, Michael." Catrin tossed her flowing mane.

"Don't want to? But, Cat darling, you must. He's so troubled, he may die. He's been ridden half to death, and surely to God, whoever it was had a mind to kill him!"

"I'm sorry, Michael," Catrin spoke softly, "but not now. Please understand."

"I do not! I do not! You'll come with me! I need you!" His attempt to excite the affection she had so recently felt for him was disastrous, for his voice rose to an hysterical shriek.

"Leave her alone, boy," Evan said. It was a challenge. Gwyn knew that this was not Nain's poor, wounded creature. He was triumphant, his few words filled with quiet menace.

Michael stood very still. A king toppled from his throne, angry and undignified. "So your uncle's the boss now, is he?" He glared at Catrin vainly trying ridicule to move her.

"He's not my uncle," Catrin declared.

The significance of her remark was too much for Michael McGoohan. He walked away from Catrin, muttering curses about older men.

The soldier ignored his insults; instead he singled out Gwyn for a special greeting. "How are you, Gwyn Griffiths?" he said with a thoughtful smile.

"I'm well," Gwyn replied.

"And did you find your toy?"

"It was not a toy," Gwyn said meaningfully. But he could not fathom the bright glance that followed this so he turned from Evan and called to Michael, "I'll come and see your Glory!"

"Let me come." Nia leaped after him.

"Clear off, both of you!" Michael made a futile gesture with his arm and began to run.

The children were not put off. They dogged the Irishman. "I know about horses," Gwyn called after him. This was a lie but Gwyn felt that if he saw Glory it might, in some way, help him understand what sort of ghosts had frightened the horse.

Michael ignored them for a while but as they insisted on pursuing him, he slowed his pace and allowed them to fall into step beside him. He needed them, after all. He needed someone to share his trouble for he would be a lonely man without his Catrin. He was still a stranger in Pendewi, even after two years, and being well-off and slightly arrogant, was not welcome everywhere. But now Gwyn was afraid for him.

Just outside the town they turned through a white gate, and descending a graveled slope, soon found themselves in an avenue of giant beech trees where rhododendrons spread like a dark curtain excluding the outside world. They had entered another kingdom: a usurped kingdom, Gwyn thought wryly, and wondered if he had inherited the thought from Nia's prince.

A breeze loosened the dying leaves and they fluttered like tiny fragments of topaz across their path, heralding the approach to the McGoohans' grand house; too grand for an ordinary doctor, but Dr. McGoohan's wife had money and was descended, so Michael boasted, from the ancient kings of Munster.

The house was built of gray stone. It was beautifully symmetrical with long Georgian windows, sixteen on each of the two floors. Two huge oak columns supported the slim porch roof, and the heavy black door was decorated with a worn pattern of scrolls and flowers. It was a Welsh home, four centuries old; a refuge for Welshmen, Gwyn found himself thinking. The McGoohans did not belong there, and again he realized he had caught the drift of ancient enmity that had very briefly flared in Evan Llŷr's remarkable blue eyes.

Michael led them across the front of the house, over a gritty driveway that crunched and rolled under their sneakered feet. Somewhere inside, his sister, Mary, played Bach on the grand piano, not half so well as Catrin. And then they were walking down a moss-grown path to the stables.

The top of Glory's stable door was open, the lower half remained closed. Michael would not let them in. They stood in the warm, cobbled yard, looking into the darkness, and the sunshine all about them made a chilling contrast with the deathly gloom of Glory's stable.

The big horse was covered in a blanket. His eyes were open; they could see a glint of white, but the rest of him was just an endless sound in the dark, a reproachful groan that rose and fell on his every breath.

"What happened?" Nia asked fearfully.

"Someone rode him," Michael murmured into the oppressive air. "Rode him all night, God knows where. There were thorns in his hair and mountain flowers. They rode him on to his knees, kicked him until he was more dead than alive."

"But who . . . ?" she began.

"I won't be the one to accuse," Michael groaned. "It has to be a madman!"

Gwyn stepped away, into the light where the sun might help him sort out a nightmare. "It's terrible," he said. "I'm sorry!" He felt an inexplicable guilt.

"Will he die?" Nia breathed.

Michael shrugged helplessly, and his voice broke as he said, "I don't know." Then tears came into his eyes and he folded his arms along the stable door and laid his head upon them.

"Come away, Nia!" Gwyn grasped her sleeve. They must leave Glory in the safe quiet where he might recover.

Nia seemed reluctant to leave the young man who had once been everything to her sister, but whose power had been so publicly damaged. Clearly embarrassed by his emotion she had to move closer to Michael so that, perhaps, he might know that he was not entirely alone.

"Nia!" Gwyn said quietly.

And this time she came with him, across the driveway and

into the shadowy lane again, and only then could Gwyn bring himself to question her.

"You never answered when I asked about your cousin," he said. "You put me off with guesses about fairy-tale princes but I want to know more, Nia!"

"Why?" She stopped and faced him, hands on hips. "Why all the questions?" She stamped her foot. "You're hounds, all of you!"

"I'm only concerned," he said gently. "He seems so . . . strange!"

She sighed and contemplated the bright leafy arches above her.

"No one has seen him for ten years," Gwyn prodded.

Nia considered the branches for a while in her irritating airy-fairy way then, almost by chance, hit upon an answer that was more than adequate. "Evan's father is not really a Llŷr," she said. "He's my mother's half brother. So there'd be no inbreeding if we married him."

"Marry? Evan and who?" Gwyn asked, incredulous.

"I don't know, any of us, Nerys, Catrin — me!"

"You?" he glared at her. "That man's old enough to be your father, and Catrin's!"

She ignored these observations. She had more to offer. "He had a brother called Emrys. He was fierce and brave, and when he was eight, he fell out of a tree and died, and Evan, who was gentle before, suddenly became just like Emrys."

Gwyn quickened his pace. He needed this history yet dreaded it.

She hopped beside him and said, close to his ear, "He was in Belfast and dreadfully wounded but — he doesn't have any scars!"

They emerged onto the main road and Gwyn closed the white gate behind them. Now it was Nia who ran eagerly forward and Gwyn who hung back, frightened of betraying his suspicion if he met the soldier.

But the black-and-bronze car had gone and Evan Llŷr was not in the house. He had left with Catrin, on one of his mysterious "trips of remembrance," as Betty Lloyd called them. Instead, they found Gwyn's uncle Idris and his cousin Emlyn in the kitchen. There was a stifled atmosphere in the room, the kind that follows an accident or death. Uncle Idris looked as if he hadn't been able to wake himself out of a very bad dream.

"Dad's been visiting the police," Emlyn explained, "and we stayed to give you a lift home."

"Thanks," Gwyn said, "but police? Why?"

Emlyn looked at his father, but Idris seemed unable to mention his problem.

"Someone broke into your uncle's studio, Gwyn," Mrs. Lloyd told him. "The unicorn was broken."

"Mutilated!" Idris roared, suddenly awake. His furious lion's eyes narrowed. "It was deliberate, careful mutilation!"

"How?" Nia asked, not understanding.

"With an ax," Idris said slowly. "Quite small, I'd say, and precise. They defiled my creature. Hacked at its ears, its eyes, and its tail; cracked my unicorn's lovely gold eyes."

The unicorn was the artist's favorite work. Marked "Not for

sale," it stood in his studio window, its magical presence brightening the gloomiest of damp Welsh days. That it should be so dreadfully disfigured was too much for Nia. She leaped protectively toward Idris. He had always been her friend. "Why?" she cried.

"Why?" Idris repeated patting her hand, as helpless and confused as she.

His studio, high on the hill road that led out of Pendewi, had once been a chapel. But Idris had decorated it with silver and gold, pink and blue, in a flamboyant gesture that had once caused suspicion and resentment in the town. Now, however, his beautiful work, his paintings and brightly carved creatures, had earned him respect and admiration. No one who passed the chapel on their way into Pendewi did so without a tingle of excitement, a feeling that, somehow, they were stepping into another world, for the unicorn held their gaze. Setting his hooves upon an invisible mountain, he seemed to be declaring that fairy tales could, after all, be true.

"It was drunks, probably," Iestyn muttered. "Who else would do a thing like that?"

"Vandals!" Betty put in. "What will they do next?"

"No," Idris told them calmly. "Not vandals, not drunks either. It was like," he sighed, "a ritual. Don't ask me how I know, but I felt the deed still in there. I could smell it."

A chorus of subdued and anxious murmurs broke out. They were all, in their way, trying to dissuade Idris from his terrible conviction.

But Gwyn, clinging to the door like someone drowning,

knew it to be true. The voices throbbed in his head, tunelessly, like a warning drummed through time. Careless magician that he was, he had failed. The demon was free again! Visions of faces that he loved peeped in at him, through the dark. Who would the madman choose next? He had destroyed so many that first time, more than a thousand years ago. Would he repeat himself? And then Gwyn thought of Nia's prince, his pale face, his perplexing summer-sea eyes and empty fingers, and he gave a remorseful little sob that caused his friends to shiver and turn in his direction.

CHAPTER SIX
Jealousy

WHEN GWYN AND THE LLEWELYNS LEFT NUMBER SIX THEY exchanged glances with no one, but it seemed to Nia that they were silently supporting one another in a manner that united them. She tried to catch Gwyn's eye but he would not look at her. News of the unicorn seemed to have alarmed him as much as the Llewelyns. She wanted to know why. Why had he hurried away as though an apparition had reared up in their cozy front room?

Mrs. Lloyd held back the evening meal and they waited for Catrin and Evan. No one knew where they had gone. At last the family began to eat uneasily, expecting an interruption at any moment. Mr. Lloyd was irritable, his stomach had lost its rhythm, he said.

Nerys blinked and peered. She'd left her glasses somewhere and she was wearing lipstick, the first time she'd done either of these things as far as Nia could remember. She wondered what had tempted her oldest sister to do something so unlikely.

It was dark when they heard the familiar roar of the black-and-bronze car. Catrin came into the kitchen with Evan close behind. They were hungry; they had not eaten. The sea had delayed them, Catrin said. The tide had been out and they had wandered across the empty sand until they had reached the water. They had removed their shoes and socks and splashed their feet in the waves, and when they had turned back, the lights were just coming on in Aberdovey.

"It was like magic," Catrin said. Her eyes looked electric. She stared at the plate of food her mother put before her, toyed with a fork, and replaced it. She could not eat. She wasn't hungry after all.

Evan ate slowly. Nia, making a pretense of tidying kitchen drawers, watched him. She found it reassuring to see him eat. It made him accessible.

"I wish you hadn't stayed out quite so long," said Mrs. Lloyd. "Your music exam is coming up soon, Catrin." Then, almost as an apology, "I suppose the sea air does you good, though!"

"Course it does, Mom," Catrin said too brightly. "And the water was so warm. I've never seen Aberdovey so . . . beautiful."

Nia pictured two figures, standing very close on a shining stretch of sand: dark silhouettes touching, then folding together, the taller bending over the other just like they did in movies. An uncomfortable knot formed in her stomach.

"Shouldn't you be in bed?" Catrin asked suddenly. And Nia, startled, dropped the drawer, scattering its contents, paper doilies, plastic bags, and clothespins, all over the floor.

"Oh, Nia, she's right." Mrs. Lloyd sighed irritably. "Look at the time. You'll be in trouble if your dad catches you."

No chance of that, Nia thought, scrabbling on the floor. She could hear the television in the next room. The game had just started. There would be another half hour to engross him.

Evan bent down to help her. He smelled of the sea and there was sand on his jeans. He put a clothespin into her hand, gently closing her fingers over it, making her look at him. "Next time I'll take you," he said quietly. "I promise!" His smile was secretive and she noticed that the chestnut streaks in his hair had multiplied; they burned through the black like tiny living flames.

Evan withdrew his hand, and Nia reluctantly stood up. She replaced the drawer, saying quickly, "I'll go to bed now, then. *Nos da*, everyone." She kissed her mother, looked at Evan, and left the room.

"*Nos da*," they called after her. "Good night, Nia." She ran up the stairs thinking of tomorrow and the sea.

She couldn't concentrate on anything the following day. She was planning her evening trip in the black-and-bronze car. They would take slices of fruitcake, she thought, and apple juice and jelly sandwiches. She knew they were Evan's favorites. They would spread a blanket on the dunes and later wander down to the sea and she would capture the magic that Catrin had found. As for standing close, she would leave that for a while, she thought, until she was tall enough to do justice to such an event. She never doubted that Evan would stay forever, or at least return to them for every vacation.

After school she ran almost all the way home, passing the waiting bus where Gwyn watched her progress with interest from his high window seat. Nia had always been one to linger, dreaming on the hill road.

The car was there, outside the house. Evan would be waiting for her. She sprang, breathless, into the kitchen and began to gather her picnic. She was adding half a loaf to the pile when her mother came in and exclaimed, "What are you doing, dear? Can't you wait for dinner?"

"I'm out for dinner, Mom," Nia said happily. "Evan's taking me today."

"Taking you where?"

"To the sea, Mom, like he did Catrin."

"I don't think so, Nia. He's not here!"

"But the car, Mom. The car is there," Nia said, a little pang of misgiving beginning to gnaw at her.

"The car maybe, but Evan is out." Mrs. Lloyd looked hard at her daughter. "What did Evan say, Nia, to make you think he'd take you?"

"He said that it was my turn," she said quietly. "He meant it, Mom, I know he did."

"Well . . ." Betty's mouth closed in a thin line. It was difficult to determine what she felt. "We'll wait and see," she said.

So Nia left her incomplete bundle on the table and went to change. She refused to believe that she was not going to have her journey so she chose her clothes carefully: her thickest sweater, creamy Aran wool handed down from Catrin but still her favorite, black jeans, and pale new sneakers. Then she took up a position on the landing where she would be the first to claim Evan when he came through the front door.

The boys were already in the kitchen scrambling for chips and lemonade.

Nerys, coming in late from the library, saw Nia on her perch and asked, "How is Catrin?"

"I don't know," Nia replied. "Is she ill?"

"Came home at lunchtime," Nerys said. "She looked awful."

Nia gave a strangled little "Oh!" Her eyes pricked and she chewed her lip to distract her tears of suspicion. "She's not at home now." Her sisters' bedroom door was open and she could see that the room was empty.

Nerys looked up, then went briskly into the kitchen. There was a commotion. Raised voices. Mrs. Lloyd ran through the hall followed by Nerys. They both went into the shop. Nia watched the door and listened. Loud conversation in the shop. Mr. Lloyd emerged in a bloody apron. "Are you sure, girl?" he said over his shoulder, then seeing Nia, commanded. "Look in Catrin's room, see if she's there, Nia. Look in all the rooms!"

Nia obeyed. She looked swiftly and calmly into every upstairs room, certain that Catrin was not alone, wherever she was, and was quite safe from kidnappers.

"No," she called. "Catrin's not here."

Mr. Lloyd was reaching for the telephone, his wife was pulling off her apron when the front door opened and Catrin sailed in. She was breathless but hardly unwell. Her hair was tumbled, her eyes wide, her face all smiles.

Very clever, Nia thought, *to make an entrance just in time, before a fuss is made and police are sent searching in the hills.*

Her sister was swept into the kitchen with questions and

complaints. "Where've you been, girl?" "Why didn't you say where you were going?" "Why did you leave school so early?" "Are you sick?"

The boys scuttled out before they could be included in the trouble that was brewing. Treats might be withheld. The television banned. But Nia, plunging through their retreat, heard Catrin object in a shrill voice. "I'm sixteen now. I'm not a child who has to tell everything. I went for a walk. I went for a walk, a walk, a walk, right?"

To Nia this disdainful repetition was proof of her sister's guilt. She wanted to know more. Trying to provoke her parents into further questioning, she asked innocently, "Were you alone?"

Her mother cast her an agitated look. "It's none of your business, Nia!"

Temporarily rebuffed, Nia left the argument and went to take up her post on the stairs. She met Evan in the hall. She was angry now. Angry with everyone, especially Evan. "I'm ready," she said defiantly.

He looked exceptionally handsome: windswept and buoyant. "Very nice," he murmured abstractedly.

"You said you would take me to the sea," she furiously reminded him. "Remember?"

"Ah," he said. "Ah, yes." And then, shaking his head in a suddenly thought-out explanation, "The car's not running right, Nia. It needs to be fixed."

"You've had all day," she said, unable to stem the deliberate rudeness.

He hardly noticed her tone. "I've been . . . preoccupied," he told her. "Problems to solve."

"I suppose you've been walking off your 'problems' with a friend!" She glowered at him, hating herself.

The wonderfully carefree expression vanished. "Ridiculous child," he said roughly.

She dropped down onto the top stair. Chastened. He strode past her into his room, not giving her the satisfaction of a slammed door, as a friend would have done, but closing it firmly behind him.

Nia brooded on the darkened stair. She was hungry for descriptions, information, anything that would give her a picture of Catrin's mysterious afternoon. She would waylay her sister. Get at the truth. When Catrin came out of the kitchen and began to mount the stairs, Nia deliberately set herself in the center.

"Nia." Catrin sighed. "Let me pass."

Nia stood aside but followed Catrin into the room she shared with Nerys. Her sister did not object, but Nia ventured no farther than the door. She stood with her back against it, ready to attack. She envied her sisters. They had made their room so pretty, painting the walls creamy yellow to match all the old pine furniture they had moved from Tŷ Llŷr. They had stripped and relaquered chests and cupboards, burning themselves with paint remover sometimes, chafing their fingers on sandpaper, reeling from the fumes but determined to re-create the bygone age that beckoned from the pages of glossy magazines. Nerys had even forbidden posters, instead she had begged samplers and flower paintings from ancient aunts, and hung them around the room.

"You're so lucky," Nia said, but her sister would not respond to this. She stood beside the window, looking out. Michael hadn't been seen for a week but Catrin still seemed unable to break her habit of watching for him. *Perhaps, after all,* Nia thought, *Catrin had been ill at school.* She knew that her parents would have asked the usual questions about time and place. These did not interest her. She wanted to get at events. Ruthless and daring, she challenged, "Has he kissed you?"

Catrin turned into the room. "Kissed?" she repeated.

"Evan? Has he? Has he?"

"Shh! What if he has?"

"No," Nia cried. "Not *that* way!"

Catrin approached her. "He's not a goblin," she said coldly. "I'm not bewitched, see!" She stretched her long pale fingers toward Nia, then flipped her hands over, palms upward, like a baby who has cleverly hidden a forbidden sweet.

"Has he?" Nia whispered.

"I'll never tell," Catrin taunted, launching herself into a series of sad and frantic giggles.

Nia fled.

✳ ✳ ✳

October broadened into a month of extremes. Frosty nights and warm, bright days lit by the violent colors of dying leaves. But the mountain chestnut was more colorful that year than any other tree. So startlingly splendid were its leaves that, from a distance, it appeared to blaze like an enchanted fire above the wreaths of evening mist.

And Evan Llŷr's luxuriant hair was growing longer. He seemed unable to comb it into any conventional shape. A mass of red and black framed his narrow face so that he took on an unreal, fairy-tale appearance. The superstitious were alarmed. Nia, forgiving everything, was entranced, for it seemed to confirm her belief that Evan was, indeed, a hero from the Celtic past. She felt as though by recognizing him she had breathed life into the troubled prince she had welcomed on that stormy day.

It was Nain Griffiths who gave Evan the name of Chestnut Soldier. On one of her rare visits to town she had met him striding down the High Street and boldly reintroduced herself, remarking on his hair and its resemblance to the flaming chestnut tree. And he had laughed his deep wild laugh and swept her into number six for tea. Nia was amazed to see how girlish Gwyn's grandmother became in Evan's company. She would not leave until she had extracted a promise from him to visit her.

Others did not feel so comfortable about Evan Llŷr. He was seen too much with Catrin Lloyd, a girl young enough to be his daughter. His hair was too long for a soldier. When would he return to the army? What was his past?

At school, girls pestered Nia for information about him. But Gwyn Griffiths and Emlyn Llewelyn were the worst. They wanted to know everything. Where the soldier went, and how he behaved when he returned. Why his hair was turning red.

How Catrin felt and why she was so pale now and so very slender. And was the soldier ever angry or violent?

Because she needed these two to be her friends, she told them she would watch her cousin and report. She would have watched without being asked. And every time she saw Evan and her sister walking together or laughing secretly, she would try to ignore the painful twist inside her and forgive him, always trusting in his promise that one day it would be her turn to be his companion by the sea.

By now the twins had given up trying to draw Evan into their games. They had hoped for a swaggering soldier, a violent man whose stories they could boastfully repeat. They felt cheated. Evan was a romantic who spent time only with their sister and who excited the female population of Pendewi for reasons they did not understand. Sometimes Nia would hear them arguing with Iolo who would always champion Evan. Alun felt himself to be above the quarrel but tended to side with the twins. No one seemed to notice Iolo's increasing distress; the way he would hide his face behind his hands as though by obstructing his view of the family, he could prevent them from recognizing him. Sometimes they would discover his toys in strange places: in his mother's drawers, behind the old dresser, inside the piano. Even when Mr. Lloyd found a toy garage in the freezer, he merely thought it another of Iolo's little idiosyncrasies.

Rehearsals for the Christmas Concert began. This year it was to be excerpts from Fauré's *Requiem.* The Male Voice Choir, the High School Orchestra, and half their relatives were roped in for the most ambitious project yet attempted. Every evening, music filled the valley from the church, the school, and the community center. Siwan Davis had been chosen to sing solo soprano and in order to achieve perfection she spent all her spare time listening to a tape of Victoria de los Angeles. Long after dusk, *"Pie Jesu"* issued from the open windows of the Davis's hill farm. It might have been this wistful accompaniment to the autumn that made it so unforgettable.

One afternoon Mr. and Mrs. Bryn Davis came into the butcher's shop. Bryn was a friend of Iestyn's and a good customer. Bryn liked Iestyn's meat. Besides his daughter, Siwan, he had a son, Dewi, whom nobody liked. Dilys, Bryn's wife, vied with Mrs. Bowen for the position of most informed busybody; she was never one to withhold advice or practical help. The Davises came into the shop just before closing time and were taken through the house to see Mrs. Lloyd. There began a low and earnest conversation in the kitchen.

Nia, overcome with curiosity, burst in on them, saying through the sudden taut silence, "I forgot my homework." She sidled behind Mr. Davis to a pile of newspapers on the dresser where she had planted her books, and then left the room.

"Shut the door, Nia!" her mother called after her, and Nia meekly replied, "Yes, Mom!" However, she had perfected a method of clicking the door shut and then immediately opening it a fraction. The adults, reassured by the first click, began to resume their conversation, never noticing the narrow crack through which Nia, hidden by the door, was listening.

"You're not worried then, Betty?" Dilys Davis continued where she'd been interrupted.

"Well, as I said . . ." Mrs. Lloyd began.

"You should be, Betty!" Mr. Davis broke in. "If it was my daughter . . . !"

"It's innocent, I'm sure," said Dilys. "But people talk, and it's not nice, Betty. Not right, I mean, for Catrin's sake."

"Can't you do anything, Iestyn?" Mr. Davis asked. "It's a man's duty."

Mr. Lloyd's chair squeaked on the tiled floor. He stood up, paced toward the window. "It's difficult, Bryn. He's a relative, see, and recuperating — had a terrible time just lately. His family's in Australia and he has nowhere else to go. The other cousins are all gone from Wales; they are in England now . . ."

"And he had to come back to Wales," Betty added softly.

"What happened out there in Northern Ireland?" Dilys Davis inquired, her quiet tone hardly disguising an unpleasant eagerness.

"Well, from what we can gather," Betty Lloyd reluctantly began, "it was a routine search for arms, no danger expected. Evan sent his platoon into a warehouse, I think it was, then suddenly there was this explosion and Evan rushed in. The radio operator tried to stop him, he said it was crazy and not the right thing to do at all, but Major Llŷr had to reach his men. He brought two out, horribly burned they were, and then went in again when the whole place went up like a . . . like a . . ."

"Wired like a cage, they said," Iestyn explained dramatically. "Four bombs in all. They didn't stand a chance. Then, after, when the fire was out, they found our major under a pile of girders, not a mark on him!"

"A miracle!" Dilys breathed.

"A hero!" Betty added.

"Oh, I remember now," Mr. Davis declared, banging the table. "It was in the papers, like a cauldron they said it was, and only one man left alive. He was in a coma for days. They never released his name. My, I never realized it was him!"

"We didn't either," Betty said. "He wouldn't speak of it. But Iestyn wrote to his regiment, just to make sure, you know, of what his accident had been. They'd kept his name out of the papers because it was all too extraordinary, a mystery!"

Outside the door, Nia was getting a cramp, yet she didn't dare move. She wondered when her father had written that letter. When had he become suspicious?

"The army doesn't like mysteries," Bryn said gravely, and his wife excited by the talk added, "His hair, all streaked red like that, it has to be the shock!"

"It must be!" her husband echoed.

"The shock," Iestyn agreed. "So we must have sympathy. And Catrin, well, perhaps she helps. She's a kind girl, and sensitive!"

Nia began to tiptoe away. Filled with this new knowledge of her cousin, her mind raced back to that first day, when her prince had come to them out of his long sleep. She did not watch her step and tripped on the stairs. Books tumbled out of her arms and slipped into the hall. She turned to retrieve them just as the front door opened and a gust of wind sent the pages into a frantic flutter, while Evan stepped in among them and stood looking down at her.

Without exchanging a word, they gathered the books together

and put them in a pile on the stairs. Nia found herself sitting beside Evan on the second stair, and couldn't stop herself from asking, "Will you take me, this time, Evan, to the sea?"

He stared at her for a moment, smiled and said, almost savagely, "Yes, I darn well will!"

"Now?"

"Right now. Get your coat."

She hurried upstairs, hardly able to believe her luck. When she came down again they were all crowding into the hall. Dilys Davis, seeing Evan in a new light, was gazing almost shyly at him while he said, "I'm taking Nia for a ride, Betty. Is that all right with you?"

"Nia?" Betty asked, surprised.

"Yes, me this time," Nia said, childishly triumphant.

"We'll see you at rehearsal then, Iestyn," Mr. Davis reminded his friend of his duty to the Male Voice Choir. Then he steered his wife toward the door, nodding respectfully at Evan, before stepping into the street.

Mrs. Lloyd buttoned Nia's jacket fussily. "You won't be too long now!" She addressed herself to Evan. "You'll be back for supper?"

He answered indirectly, "I'll take good care of her, Betty." He took Nia's hand, and stepping into the street, they approached the car together, like conspirators.

"Do you like to travel with the top down?" he asked her, and when Nia nodded, he jumped into the driver's seat and pressed a switch, turning his strange car into a gleaming roofless chariot.

Nia stood on the curb, almost afraid. If she entered the prince's chariot would she turn into something her family would not recognize?

"Hurry! Before the sun sets," he commanded. And to reassure her, he climbed out and opened a door. "Into the back," he said. "Where children are safe!"

She grimaced and got in. Evan laughed and said, "Time will fly, Nia. You'll soon be old enough to sit beside me!"

Like Catrin does, she thought, and said, "Let's make time fly now!"

The engine growled into action and they sailed up High Street, passing Gwyn Griffiths on the bridge. He was talking to Alun and Emlyn. Two boys returned her vigorous waving but Gwyn looked glum and seemed to shake his head.

"We'll go to Harlech," Evan declared. "Where it all began."

She did not ask what he meant but pressed herself into the seat and half closed her eyes, enraptured with the smell of leather, the freshness of the wind, and the whirl of mountains, sheep, and sky.

They traveled in silence for nearly an hour and then came within sight of the sea. A huge sun balanced on the edge of the horizon, and against the mountains, the great castle was defined by shadows.

The road that led to the castle on its giant rock was deliciously steep and narrow. There were no visitors in the parking lot; they had the place to themselves. But the castle was closed so they stood by the southeastern tower where a statue of the dying King Bendigeidfran turned away from the sea. Behind the king on his weary horse lay a dead boy: Gwern, the king's nephew, a victim of the mad Efnisien.

Nia had forgotten the statue and remembered only the view: Mount Eryri, the rugged towers that swept toward the sky and the delicate blue line of the Llyn peninsula curving into the sea. When she had been younger, she purposely put sad things out of her mind; she had been prone to nightmares.

"It's so old, this castle," she murmured.

"No," Evan retorted. "Not so old!"

"But . . ." she began.

"It wasn't here," he said abruptly, "when they were." He half turned his head toward the statue but wouldn't look at it. Then he paced away from the dying king and added, "There was only the rock."

"Oh!" Hugging herself against the wind, Nia twirled about trying to turn the landscape into a wild kaleidoscope. At last she came to rest beside him. He would not even glance at the scenery that so delighted her but remained very still, glaring across the sea. In spite of the wind, beads of sweat glittered on his face and she wondered what mirage could be there, beyond the horizon, that had suddenly called up so much wrath. Her prince had slipped away again and left a demon in his place, his wild hair ruffled like some mythic beast, his windblown jacket surging darkly all around him.

Adrift between the elements and this grim stranger she felt afraid. She wanted to bring him back but could not think how to do it. At last she ventured, "What is it like — to be a soldier?"

He turned to her, very slowly, and replied, "It depends on who you are!"

"But being who you are?"

He seemed to be sizing her up, deciding if she was worthy of a true answer. Then all at once he leaned toward her and softly confided, "Glorious!"

Astonished she mumbled, "But . . ."

"Glorious," he repeated. For a moment his smile was wicked and his eyes mirrored colors that were not apparent in their surroundings, brimstone and flame-green. She moved away from him and watched him looking across the sea again. He was far away now, somewhere where it troubled and excited him. Then he thrust his fingers through his wild hair as though he were trying to rub away the rage. "A soldier is a hero to half the world," he murmured uneasily. "The others," he shrugged, "would rather be without us!" This time his smile was sorrowful. He was almost her quiet prince again. "Let's go down to the beach," he said.

They climbed into the car and sped down the narrow cliff road, then over the railroad tracks and down to the sea. The sun had almost set but the clouds were bright and reflected gold glittered over the sand. They left the car on a shoulder of the road, then, abandoning their socks and shoes, plunged through the dunes to the beach.

Nia immediately ran to the water. She splashed a path along the tidal line of shells and seaweed, aware that Evan was watching, his hands in his pockets and almost happy again. He began to march across the sand, and Nia ran in front of him and around him, laughing and leaping backward sometimes, in a little dance that had a pattern to it, and because his strides were measured and unhesitant, their movements took on the shape of a strange ritual that they might have always known.

When they climbed back across the dunes, the wind, singing in the tall grass, flung handfuls of sand at them, and Nia had to keep her mouth closed tight against her giggles.

She insisted that she wasn't cold and so, with the roof open to the dark sky and darker mountains, they sped away from the sea and the colored clouds, and as all light faded, she watched the headlights beaming them forward through a bright tunnel. Swathes of mist drifted across the road and when she looked back, the mountains had vanished. Nothing was familiar. Huddled against Evan's shoulder, Nia fancied that she was plunging into the Otherworld in a war chariot driven by some fantastic legendary god or chieftain. She did not mind that her time with the prince had not lasted as long as her sister's, that certain events might have been omitted from her adventure. Evan had given her enough to puzzle over and to cherish.

❄ ❄ ❄

At number six dinner was waiting for them. Nia entered the kitchen with a challenging stare, meant especially for Catrin. Her sister deliberately avoided her glance, but Nia, watching closely, saw a listening expression cross her face when Evan came in. Catrin would not look at him.

Nia had intended to boast of the warm beach and the sunset. She had thought that she would tell about Mount Eryri and her dance beside the water but she found that she could not. It had become something special that could not be shared. And when her father asked how their journey had been and had they seen the sea, she could only answer, "It was great!"

The atmosphere was strained. The younger children had eaten earlier and where the twins' noisy chatter would have been, there was an uncomfortable emptiness. Alun tried a few jokes. Evan smiled and Mr. Lloyd laughed seconds too late. Nerys had nervously applied makeup to her long thin face. It was a disastrous experiment; the color was wrong and she looked like an unsuccessful clown. Everyone wondered what had possessed her, but she seemed so sadly ill at ease that no one could bear to ridicule her efforts.

After supper when the household had dispersed, Nia heard a monotonous and desultory tune coming from the piano in the front room. Catrin seemed unable to perform. Nia opened the door and peering around it asked, "Can I listen?"

Hunched over the piano, Catrin said nothing.

Nia slipped quietly into a chair. Catrin toyed with the keys and then thrust her hands across the piano, pounding out discordant ugly chords. She was too musical to bear the sound for long, however, and gradually brought her fingers under control until the notes softened into a tune again. It was then that Nia became aware of the high treble accompaniment of sobbing. "I can't play anymore." Catrin wept quietly. "It's beyond me!"

Nia stood up, ready to leave the room. Her sister's distress seemed too private. But as she touched the door Catrin said, "Glory is dead!"

"No!" Nia cried. "Oh no," and she ran to Catrin who flung

her arms around her, sobbing, "Michael blames me, I don't know why. He's so cruel now. Won't speak to me. And he's seeing Lluned Price every day."

Astonished that Catrin should be sharing this news with her, Nia marveled, nevertheless, at her sister's self-deception. Surely Catrin must know what the town, and therefore, Michael, thought. She had been seen so often with Evan Llŷr. She had refused Michael when he needed her. Surely he was a boy of the past. But perhaps it hurt that he had chosen someone else. It was all such a puzzle. As Catrin sobbed against her shoulder, Nia resolved that she would never find herself in such a quandary. She would love always and forever, to the very end.

"Don't tell them." Catrin brushed her wet cheeks with the back of her hand.

"Course not," Nia said. She stood at Catrin's side a moment longer, studying the tortuous black patterns of her sister's music. Catrin began to fumble with the keys again and Nia wondered how she could avoid the age of sixteen when it was possible to be hurt by so many things at once: a dead horse, a boy's rejection, music that you couldn't play.

When she let herself out of the room, Catrin had begun to draw something almost tuneful from the piano.

All that stuff she told me was only part of the truth, Nia thought. *It was Evan taking me to the sea, that was the real hurt, but it came out as all sorts of other things.*

She climbed the stairs wondering if Evan had left the house. What would he be doing if he was in his room? Did he read? Write? She had never seen him with a book. She glanced toward his door. It gave nothing away. The house was exceptionally quiet; even the boys' voices were low. She began to mount the narrow flight of stairs that led to the top bedrooms: her parents' and the room she shared with Iolo and Bethan.

Bethan was asleep in her crib but in the corner, where a soft light glowed on the sloping roof, Iolo lay in a tense huddle. Nia knew he was awake. She crept over to him and touched his shoulder. "Go away," said a muffled voice from the mound of blankets.

"What's the matter, Iolo?"

He turned on his back and glared at her, his eyes red-rimmed with drying tears.

"What is it? Should I call Mom?" Nia asked. She had little confidence in her nursing abilities.

Iolo shook his head.

"Should I turn out the light?"

Another shake of the head, then screwing up his face he blurted out, "He promised me. He promised to take me!"

"Who?" She knew, of course, but had to play for time while she thought of a way to settle him.

"Evan. He said he'd take me in the car, one day. But he never does. It's always Catrin, and now it's you. He said I could walk with him, but he never waits. And he never talks to me now."

Nia didn't know how to comfort her brother. "Perhaps you're too shy," she suggested. "Ask him about the car tomorrow. I'll help you!"

Iolo stared at her searchingly. "OK." He yawned, burrowed into a comfortable position, and closed his eyes.

Nia undressed, turned out the light, and got into bed. She lay very still, listening intently for sounds from the room beneath. But there were none. She fell asleep and dreamed that she was riding in a chariot through a cloud of larks that whirled about her head like the butterflies in Idris Llewelyn's studio. Distant hoofbeats drifted into her dream and fixed themselves in her head, edging out the smoother singing sounds. In her confused and drowsy state she wondered if it could be the poor broken unicorn, or the spirit of black Glory come to take her to the Otherworld.

All at once she was wide awake and the hoofbeats had rolled out of her dream and into the night of the street. She must see this phantom for herself.

Kneeling on the dressing table, she reached up to the high dormer window, opened it carefully, and peered down into the street. The horse, or whatever it was, was coming closer. Suddenly its speed increased and it galloped across her narrow line of vision. A wild white horse, a stallion perhaps who had left the mountain herd or been stolen from it by the dark rider on his back; a man who wore something bright that billowed around him like a cloud.

Nia closed the window and went back to bed. "A ghost," she told herself. "Farmers do not wear cloaks and gallop around at night." She thought of telling this story at breakfast, knowing very well that she would not tell anyone.

❊ ❊ ❊

On Saturday mornings number six was always more than half empty. Alun went to soccer practice, and the twins went to cheer him on. Catrin had extra music lessons with Miss Olwen Oliver. Nerys was always in the library. Mr. Lloyd was in his shop, his wife in the kitchen singing to Bethan while she made pies, and Iolo drew pictures of animals and tall, colored houses. This Saturday, Evan had left the house before anyone was up. His note on the kitchen table told them that he would be away for a day and a night.

Alone in her high bedroom Nia reflected on the events that had crowded too fast into the recent hours: her visit to the sea, her sister's tears, the phantom horse. She must share some of these secrets soon, she thought, with someone she could trust, or they would tumble out where they shouldn't.

She left the room and descended in a drifting way to the landing. She glanced down the passage. At the end, Evan's door invited her from its deep shadows. She walked slowly toward it, put her hand on the doorknob, and found herself looking through the open doorway into Evan's room. It told her nothing. Its tidiness was depressing. Only the jacket left on the back of a chair gave a clue to the room's occupant. Nia wandered into the room. It was a cool, featureless place, but in the mornings a sliver of sunlight would creep through the window. She patted the pillow, straightened the coverlet. She ran her finger along the top of the dressing table, not daring to open a drawer. He had left nothing for her to do, except perhaps tidy the jacket into smoother folds. She picked it up and must have turned it upside down, for something fell out of an inner pocket.

It lay on the pale carpet, a small dark object, wooden, an

animal without ears or tail. She knew it was Gwyn's lost horse. Holding her breath she knelt down and touched it, ready to feel the fear that Gwyn had prepared her for. But it was not a dreadful thing at all. It was light. Harmless. She threw it up, caught it, and almost laughing, passed it from one hand to another.

"Oh, Gwyn," she said to the sunshine in the air. "There's no demon here. It's empty!"

And then the fear came.

CHAPTER SEVEN

Confession

GWYN WAS ON THE MOUNTAIN WHEN HE SAW NIA AND IOLO arriving. He was gathering straw for the cattle's winter bedding, in a field that was too steep to mow. He dumped the last bundle into the trailer and began to run down the track. Nia had something to tell him at last. He had been waiting anxiously for something to jolt her out of her ridiculous loyalty to her cousin. As he ran he speculated on what could have led Nia to seek his help. His downhill race became a wild plummeting.

His visitors were already in the house when he reached the porch. He dutifully flung off his muddy boots and ran into the kitchen. The Lloyds were sitting, waiflike, at the table, waiting for hot chocolate.

"I've brought Nia and Iolo for the weekend," his mother explained as she heated milk on the stove.

"The weekend?" Gwyn noticed two bulging plastic bags beside the door. A pajama sleeve dangled, pathetically, from one. Their departure must have been hasty.

"What happened?" he asked nervously.

Nia frowned, trying to decide on an answer. "Iolo was having a hard time," she said at last.

Iolo obviously did not object to this remark. He nodded vehemently.

Gwyn was disappointed. He had hoped for something more impressive. "Why?" he asked.

"He keeps losing things and — people are being mean." She looked furtively over her shoulder and whispered, "I'll tell you the rest later."

Here was better news. *If it cannot be spoken aloud it must be interesting*, Gwyn reasoned. He joined them at the table and asked for a cup of hot chocolate. Mrs. Griffiths automatically added more milk to the saucepan. She looked as though she could not quite grasp the situation and was comforting herself with a quiet and familiar routine.

Gwyn and the Lloyds sipped their hot drinks, slowly postponing further conversation while they avoided scalding their tongues on the hot liquid.

"Perhaps you two would like to take your things to Bethan's room," Mrs. Griffiths suggested when the mugs were empty. She never said, "the room where Bethan used to sleep," because she had never relinquished the hope that, one day, her daughter would return to claim her place, although it was eight years now since Bethan had vanished.

Nia loved the room. She had once confided to Gwyn that she felt peaceful, surrounded by Bethan's dolls and clothes. It was a state that always seemed to elude Nia in her own home.

"Come on." Nia nudged her brother and made for the door.

"I'll bring a mattress for Iolo later," Mrs. Griffiths called after them.

"Iolo can share my room if he wants to," Gwyn proposed. He could not think why he had said this. Later he assumed that it was intuition.

The Lloyds stopped in their tracks. Nia astonished. Iolo round-eyed with enthusiasm. "Yes, please," he said.

"Take your stuff and put it on my bed," Gwyn told him. "I'll sleep on the mattress."

"That was kind, Gwyn," Mrs. Griffiths said when the Lloyds had gone.

"Iolo's all right," Gwyn murmured. "He's different from the twins, quieter. We'll be OK. What happened, Mom? Why are they here? Why not Alun? It's all a little sudden."

"Alun had a big game, and I don't know why those two are here, that's the truth. I was in the shop to get meat for the weekend when Nia burst in from the house." Mrs. Griffiths lowered her voice. "She looked, quite frankly, terrified. I don't know what's been going on. Poor Betty, I don't know how she manages it: eight children and I've only one to worry about."

They eyed each other but did not mention Bethan.

"Go on about Nia," Gwyn encouraged. "Why did you bring her here?"

"Well, she stared at me, I don't know, as if I were her salvation and almost yelled, '*Please*, Mrs. Griffiths, can I come and stay with you, *please, please!*' Her father looked quite put out. Well, I went into the house, and of course, Betty was very happy for Nia to come. She said Catrin needed a bit of attention, she wasn't herself, and then all at once Iolo cries out, 'Can I come, too?' And Nia said, 'Let him come,' and added all those 'pleases' again, so I couldn't refuse, could I?"

"I'm glad you didn't. Was Catrin ill?" He asked the question in an off-hand way, not wishing to appear too interested in her.

"No. But she hasn't looked well lately, and always going around with Evan . . ."

"Yes." Gwyn curtailed any discussion that might revolve around Evan Llŷr. He knew where his mother's sympathies lay.

"That poor man, his hair . . . I heard from the Davises . . ."

"Yes, yes!" Gwyn said, not waiting for a story he would have found enlightening. "I'm going to see what those two are doing."

Nia was sitting on the patchwork quilt that covered his sister's bed. She had Bethan's rag dolls in her lap and was fixing their hair. Gwyn sat beside her.

"Will she come back again?" Nia asked.

"Bethan?" Gwyn shrugged. "Perhaps. If I call her!"

"Will you?"

"No," Gwyn said and then added, regretfully, "she's happy in another place. She'll always be a child and I'm afraid if I've outgrown her, we'll have nothing left to say to each other. When she came back that other time, we were almost the same age."

Nia hugged all three dolls, sighing hugely. Gwyn laughed and said, "Come on, it's not that sad. Now tell me what happened."

"I don't know what came over me," she said. "I was so scared, I didn't know what to do. I didn't know who to tell, and then there was your mother, just like an answer to a prayer I hadn't thought of. I feel a bit silly now."

"So tell me!" Gwyn demanded.

Nia felt inside her jacket pocket and brought out the broken horse. Gwyn stared at it, almost disbelieving. "Thank goodness," he said. "Where was it?"

Nia hung her head and murmured reluctantly, "It fell out of Evan's coat."

Gwyn grabbed the horse from her. "I knew it. All the time I've known it. But I didn't want it to be true."

"You knew he had it?"

"Not just that. I know why he had it!"

"Perhaps he meant to give it back but forgot?"

Gwyn shook his head. He yawned, longing to lay his head down. It was like having flu without the pain. Just knowing he was going to have to embark on an impossibly ambitious spell exhausted him. And it would have to be soon, before the demon grew confident and completely overcame the soldier. But how could he stop him, and with what? "You realize, Nia, what has happened, don't you?" Gwyn said.

"No!"

He knew she was lying.

"That day Iolo lost the horse, and I believed I had trapped his spirit, even though we never found it. And Evan fell under the chestnut tree, and you thought he cried out, silently . . ."

"He's a poor wounded soldier," she said reproachfully.

"Listen," Gwyn cried. "That mad, black spirit was free for a while, but I caught it, Nia, in Arianwen's web. Only Evan got in the way, somehow, and now he is possessed." He peered into her averted face and made her look at him. "The dark soul of Efnisien is there, Nia, in your great prince." He almost enjoyed the way her rebellious expression began to crumple. At last she must believe him.

Defiant to the end, she muttered, "No! He's a hero. And I'll tell you why. When he was in Northern Ireland he ran into a burning warehouse to save his men; he shouldn't have done it, they said. He broke the rules. It was hopeless, you see. And they all burned to death except for him. And he had no wounds at all. It was a mystery. They never gave Evan's name to the papers because it was unnatural, I suppose. Impossible. I was outside the door when Mom told the Davises. I don't think we were supposed to know. But you see, he's a hero, not a demon."

She didn't realize that instead of contradicting Gwyn she'd given him all the proof he needed. Reasons and events whirled in his head, sorting themselves into a dreadful pattern. It was terrifying and yet exhilarating, discovering the ability to fit the pieces of a story together.

"I can see now that Efnisien has been calling to Evan for a long time," he said, "so that he could enjoy life again in the form of someone like himself. Evan's life is almost an echo of his own — a soldier, a Llŷr who is not a Llŷr, a man who is the opposite of his own brother. Nia, he even tried to sacrifice himself in a fire, but at the moment when Evan's hate matched his own, Efnisien was able to reach the soldier and save him for himself. The rest was inevitable. Hatred is a dreadful force; it makes things happen."

"But what about me?" Nia's voice called plaintively into his excited speculations. "Was I supposed to find the horse again?"

Gwyn stopped pacing and thought about that. "No," he said. "It was an accident. You went into that room because you are . . . silly about Evan."

She bristled. "Not *so* silly. I knew he was a prince!"

"Prince!" Gwyn exclaimed, exasperated. "This isn't a fairy tale, Nia. We're sliding into a real tragedy, a parallel story if you like, that might not have a happy ending. And I have to stop it, somehow. I'm the only one."

"All the same," she quietly persisted, "Efnisien was a prince."

"Huh!" was all Gwyn said. But he couldn't deny it. "Evan found the horse in the stream and would have given it to me, but I prevented that because I am an idiot. Always an idiot with my spells. Once the demon was there, safe within his soul, he hid the horse so that I could never again use it to trap him. Don't you see, Nia? It's so clear. Glory was afraid of Evan the moment he saw him. His memory was inherited from the horses Efnisien maimed. Fear of that prince had become an instinct. And the unicorn, Iolo's toy horses, they were a repetition Evan couldn't help."

"Evan didn't do those things," Nia broke in.

"Of course he did," Gwyn said roughly. "Efnisien is beginning to relive his story."

"And Catrin is Branwen," Nia said flatly.

Does Nia wish it could have been her role? Gwyn wondered.

"I believe so," he said.

"What should we do?" she asked helplessly.

Gwyn was forming an answer when the door handle rattled and Iolo's face appeared. "I'm going to help your dad with the ewes in the top field," he told Gwyn proudly.

"We're going to see my Nain, sure you don't want to come?" Gwyn asked, sure that Iolo would not.

"No way!" Iolo disappeared.

"Your Nain!" Nia had brightened immediately when Gwyn mentioned his grandmother, as though their problems were half solved already.

❋ ❋ ❋

Nain Griffiths welcomed them as a glorious excuse for a party. She wanted them to try her new poppy seed cake, her fresh apple juice, and her hazelnut cookies. Spreading all this tempting food over a lace cloth on her lawn, she brought cushions out of the house and pushed the children onto them while she hummed and twirled to show off her new three-tiered skirt. Gwyn couldn't break through her persistent cheerfulness. At last he almost shouted, "Look, Nain, we've got a problem!" and her bird-bright glance told him that she had known it all along but needed her tea party to celebrate this longed-for visit.

"Well?" she said, perching in a temporary way on the remains of a cane chair that had obviously housed many generations of mice.

But they didn't know where to begin and Nain was about to fly off for another plate when Gwyn brought the broken horse from his pocket and put it on the white cloth where it couldn't fail to catch her eye.

Arrested in mid-flight, she glared at the animal and said hoarsely, "Why have you brought *that* here, Gwydion Gwyn?"

So Gwyn told his story from the beginning, when they had walked up the mountain to admire the red kite, and Iolo had found the horse and let it fall into the stream. He left nothing out but neither he nor his grandmother had the whole picture until Nia added her part.

When she described her visit to Harlech, there were moments of terror for him, but his grandmother remained calm. He could not understand this when she must have known why Evan had glared across the Irish Sea, must have remembered that Efnisien had sailed across it, perhaps from that very spot, to fight and die for his sister, Branwen. And Nia was pitching herself back into those hours with Evan as though they were the only true and wonderful moments of her life. Women, Gwyn thought, were unfathomable.

"You're not afraid," Gwyn accused his grandmother. "Once, you could hardly bear to look at that horse. You wouldn't forgive me for setting it free four years ago. What's so different now?"

"For one thing, it isn't free!" Nain grinned in an irritating way. "This time, I know I'm not at risk!"

"You're very smug, I must say!" Gwyn exploded. He leaped up, jerking the cloth, and the broken horse gave a little jump against a cup that tinkled like a tiny warning, or so it seemed to him. The others, however, appeared to be enchanted with the incident and laughed delightedly.

"Come on, you two," Gwyn stormed. "Grow up! We're all at risk. There's a madman on the loose, lusting for glory, and murder, too, most probably."

"You're wrong, Gwyn!" Nain said, suddenly grave. "Our chestnut soldier will fight the violence he's been saddled with."

"And if he loses?"

"Then he will need your help, won't he?" she retorted. "It's your fault, boy. You bewitched that poor soldier as surely as your ancestors ensnared one another into the lives of animals. And you said that you were tired of magic!"

Gwyn ignored her last remark.

"You admit then," he said, "that we could be in for trouble. That there's danger."

"Now, now!" His grandmother set out on a little dancing journey through her orchard, flinging tuneful messages over the fields. "You think you've pinned him down, don't you?" she sang. "Foisted on that poor soldier some convenient mythical personality to suit a coincidence of horses. But do you really know, Gwydion Gwyn? Stories take a tortuous route through time. Perhaps this one isn't quite true? Yes, I began it all. I gave you the horse. I knew it was a dreadful thing. But it was you who decided it held the tortured soul of that poor prince. Did he really commit the murders ascribed to him? If he did, then he atoned for them. He was flung into the boiling cauldron, a living man, stretched himself until he broke into four parts, and his heart was broken also."

Gwyn was determined not to be impressed. "Something of

him was left," he muttered darkly. "The diabolical part. I had it kept safe and now it's on a rampage."

"Oh, la, la, la, la, la!" his grandmother trilled mockingly.

"You've been led astray!" Gwyn furiously accused her. "Why have you allowed it?"

"Because I am a woman," she replied.

"A crazy one," he said grimly. *She's lost,* he thought, *hoodwinked by a blue-eyed Llŷr. She can't help herself.* And then he told her of the fire in Northern Ireland, and Evan's part in it, how he had tried to throw his life away to save his men, and failed.

And Gwyn knew his grandmother believed at last, but although she looked anxious, it was not in the way he had hoped for. "Poor man," she murmured.

Overhead white mares' tails were racing through the blue sky, and a little wind billowed beneath the cloth. Nia caught the broken horse as it rolled onto the grass. "What shall I do with this?" she asked. "He'll know I found it."

"Let him know," Nain said. "Gwyn, soon you must show him who you are, and that you'll help him."

"Perhaps he is enjoying his new soul. He seemed lonely without one," Gwyn muttered. He was thinking that after all, he had not been entirely responsible for the change in Evan. It had begun far away, in an Irish fire.

They gathered up the cloth and the empty cups and plates and took them into the kitchen. But before Nia and Gwyn left, Nain took them into her forest of a room, where plants held sway over everything, even the furniture. Nia was commanded to relax while Gwyn cleared the table of books. Then his grand-mother produced a large deck of cards wrapped in black silk. She laid the cards on the table, facedown, in a fan shape.

"What are we going to do?" Intrigued, Nia began to count the cards.

Nain tapped her hand. "Let them be," she said. "There are seventy-eight. You must choose one. This is not the normal route to the truth, but it will serve my purpose. I may not be a wizard" — she glanced at Gwyn — "but I have my ways. Have you heard of tarot cards, Nia?"

Nia shook her head. "Is it like fortune-telling?"

"No! It is a way of seeking the truth, and thereby a solution."

Gwyn sighed. He knew the cards. They told stories, related lives, caused thought when action was needed.

"No need for that," Nain chided him. "If I am not wrong, Nia is close to the heart of this matter. If she chooses the right card, then it is she who will take our story to its happy conclusion. Now, Nia, take your time. Empty your mind and choose a card."

Gratified, but anxious not to jeopardize the proceedings, Nia made a show of closing her eyes, flexing her fingers, and biting her lip.

"That will do," Nain said sharply. "It is in your heart, Nia, not your fingers."

Nia relaxed and Gwyn found himself regarding the cards with reluctant fascination. The smooth sweep of black and gold hid pictures he'd once longed to play with. Nain would never let him. *The tarot cards must be respected,* she had told him, they should be left in peace so that they could tell their stories, do their work unhindered. What work would that be? He had been too impatient then to find out. He watched Nia stretch her hand toward the left of the fan. She was thoughtful now. Carefully she withdrew a card and handed it to his grandmother.

"I knew it." Nain lay the card face upward on the table and clasped her hands. "The chariot!"

Gwyn beheld a blue-eyed man with copper-colored curls beneath a bronze helmet. He wore a bronze breastplate over a bloodred tunic and stood in a bronze war chariot. In his left hand he held the reins of a white horse, in his right hand, the reins of a black horse. The animals appeared to differ in their preferred route. The black horse veered to the right, the white horse to the left. Behind the chariot a red desert stretched beneath a dark and stormy sky.

Gwyn observed Nia's face as it registered puzzlement and then pleasure. "Who is he?" she asked.

"You have chosen Ares the war god," Nain told her. "He embodies conflict and bloodshed. His driving force is aggression."

"That's not very pleasant for a hero," Nia remarked. "I bet he came to grief!"

"He didn't," Nain said. "The goddess Aphrodite fell in love with Ares. She loved him for his strength and vitality. A strange match, you might argue. The war god and the goddess of love. And yet what came of it?" She waited, her head on one side.

"What?" Nia asked, suddenly realizing an answer was expected.

"Harmony!" Nain told her joyfully. "They had a daughter, and her name was Harmony. Don't you see?" She lifted her hands, and her silver bracelets caught the sunlight and shimmered wonderfully. She opened her fingers and sparks flew from her jeweled rings. "Harmony!" she chanted. "Now do you understand?"

"Harmony," Nia repeated, beginning to enjoy the word. At last it dawned on her that she might have an equal share with Gwyn in determining the outcome of the story. If he must defeat demons, she could happily supply love.

There was a fizz of excitement in the air. Gwyn was uneasy. He had learned nothing from the strange experiment. His grandmother folded her cards into a neat pack and laid them gently in their black cloth. "That was very satisfactory," she said.

"We'd better go," Gwyn told her. "Iolo's back at home. I ought to keep an eye on him."

"You'll come again, won't you?" His grandmother looked suddenly anxious.

"Of course," he said.

They left the house by way of the fallow field, where Nia remarked on the number of birds that flew, complaining, out of the thistles.

"Can I come tomorrow?" she called to the tall woman, all in green, who looked like a sapling in her golden grove.

"Someone will be here," came the enigmatic reply.

"You know," said Gwyn as they strolled through the fields, "I don't think you're taking this seriously enough, Nia."

"I am," she replied earnestly. "I was really frightened when I found that horse. But Evan is wonderfully strong, your Nain has helped me to see that. I can't believe he'd do anything really wicked."

"I hope not," Gwyn said grimly. "Once I was almost persuaded that legends are not true. But I know better now. The names and places may be different, but there were princes and battles, there was jealousy and murder and terrible love, and there were magicians." He looked at his hands and added, "And they're all still here. Perhaps it's because our land is so ancient. Ghosts feel at home; they find it easy to slip into our lives like long-lost relatives."

"I don't seem to fit any story," Nia said. "I've just wandered in by accident!"

And now you're part of it, Gwyn thought. "Nain seems to believe you're as close to finding a solution as any of us!" he said.

They found Iolo sitting on the yard gate. He was bursting with pride. "I helped your dad sort out the ewes," he told Gwyn. "We've brought a hundred down from the mountain for dipping. Fly was brilliant. She kept them all together with a little help from me and Cymro."

Fly had been the Lloyds' dog once, when they had lived at Tŷ Llŷr. But they had parted with her when they went to live in Pendewi. She had lasted one miserable, whining day in the town and then came to join Cymro, the Griffiths's sheepdog.

Gwyn, Nia, and Iolo spent the rest of the day on the mountain together, searching for the red kite. The weather was hardly cooler than on that burning September day when Iolo had lost the broken horse. Now it was found. Too late. The kite did not appear for them, and Gwyn couldn't enjoy the walk. Nia, however, seemed happy, knowing that his grandmother felt so confident about her chestnut soldier.

That night Iolo refused Gwyn's offer of a bed. It was more fun, he said, to sleep on the floor. He was happy with his mattress and sleeping bag. When Gwyn came to bed, however, the younger boy was still wide awake.

As Gwyn climbed into bed he was beginning to frame a question that, he knew, had risks attached to it. He turned off the bedside light, and in the darkness, asked, "Iolo, how do you like your cousin Evan?"

What answer did he expect? Perhaps the one he received.

"I don't!" Iolo said.

"Why?"

"He was nice to me once; now he never has time. It's like I don't exist."

Gwyn was surprised by the anger. He sought to turn it to his advantage. "Will you do something for me?"

"What?" Iolo asked cautiously.

Gwyn judged that he was ready. "Will you follow your cousin for me? Watch him, but always secretly. Find out what he does and where he goes. Never let him know what you are doing, though. It could be dangerous."

"Dangerous?"

"I believe Evan broke your horses, Iolo, and my uncle's unicorn." He plunged on, aware of the effect his words had already had, "I think he was responsible for Glory's death." He had no need to fuel Iolo's dislike, but couldn't help himself.

The little boy was sitting bolt upright, staring at the pale moonlit curtains. "How could he?" he exclaimed. "He was my friend. What's happened to him?"

"I can't tell you yet," Gwyn said. "If you watch him, we'll find out. Will you do it? I'm not sure if I can trust anyone else."

Iolo was flattered. "Yes," he said, and Gwyn knew he had an ally.

"Are you allowed to use the phone?"

"If I ask," Iolo replied.

"When you've something to tell, call me after six. Say you want to see me, nothing more. I'll make the arrangements." Gwyn said this, aware of the perils of such an operation, but never dreaming how much he would regret it.

❋ ❋ ❋

On Sunday morning Emlyn and Geraint came up to the farm. They loved to lend a hand. The ewes and the weaned lambs had to be sorted, ready for dipping on Monday. The older animals were already suspicious. They remembered the smell, the stinging in their eyes and ears, the terrible taste. Idris Llewelyn would have to come and help. It needed strong hands to subdue the big rams, and at six foot three and two hundred pounds, Idris was one of the strongest men in the district.

After their work the children began to walk down to Tŷ Llŷr. They rounded the bend from where Nain's cottage could be seen, just as a dark figure emerged from her garden. For some reason they all stood quite still as the man stepped into the road. He was tall and wore a black jacket round his shoulders. He did not see them and began to walk in the opposite direction, then suddenly he turned and looked back. He didn't wave. The sun was in Gwyn's eyes and he couldn't see the man's features. Nia cried, "It's Evan!"

Gwyn laid a hand on her arm but she pulled away from him and ran down to her cousin. The four boys stood watching as the two figures disappeared into the trees that bordered the river.

Emlyn, always sensitive to Gwyn's moods, asked, "What's up?"

Iolo's eyes widened. He nudged Gwyn, enjoying their new relationship.

"It's all right, Iolo," Gwyn reassured him. "Emlyn's with us. It'll take some explaining," he told Emlyn. "Can you wait?"

Emlyn nodded. "Is Nia in trouble?" he asked.

"Not exactly." Gwyn sighed. And added, "I think I may need your help."

"My sister's crazy," Iolo said unnecessarily.

❄ ❄ ❄

Mr. Griffiths returned Nia and Iolo to their own home on Sunday afternoon. Before Iolo parted company with Gwyn he winked and gave a rather obvious thumbs-up sign.

Gwyn worried that he'd piled the drama on too thickly. Was an eight-year-old capable of such a dangerous mission?

Three days later, at six o'clock in the evening, Iolo phoned him.

"Hello, it's me!" a perilously creaky voice informed him. "Nothing's happened yet, but *he's* just gone out — alone. I'm going to follow him!"

"Iolo . . ." Gwyn began, but there was a click and the line went dead.

Gwyn stood in the dark passage wishing that somehow, through the maze of wires that had momentarily connected them, he could drag Iolo back to hear his warning. A tiny tremor rippled through the floor and a sudden wind burst through the gate, seeking out loose straw and driving it in a ghostly dance across the yard. Gwyn went into the kitchen and watched, fascinated, through the window. It was one of those unnatural winds that was up to no good.

At nine o'clock that night, his mother called up to his attic room. "Gwyn, have you seen Iolo? Betty Lloyd's on the phone. She's frantic. He left the house some time after dinner and hasn't been seen since!"

CHAPTER EIGHT
Farewell

GWYN DIDN'T KNOW HOW TO TELL HER AND SO HE CALLED
back, "No, I haven't seen Iolo." And then, suddenly, in wild
indecision, "Well . . ."

"What was that?" his mother shouted.

"Nothing," he said miserably. He'd lost his chance.

Emlyn Llewelyn had been the last person to see Iolo. He had
passed the chapel, Emlyn said, at half past six. He was alone
and appeared to be heading to the mountain.

Mrs. Lloyd phoned the police. A search party was organized:
Idris and Emlyn, Gwyn and his father, Mr. Lloyd and a few neigh-
boring farmers and their sons. Twenty men set off, on foot, to
comb the mountain fields. A bitter wind thrashed against their
faces but the rain held off and the moon was full. Clusters of stars
could be seen, glittering through the driven threadbare clouds.

It was Fly who found Iolo. Memory and her sixth sense must
have told her where to look. He had fallen into a stone quarry
that bordered the river.

Gwyn and Mr. Griffiths, attuned to Fly's whining signals,
ran to the cliff top immediately above her. Mr. Griffiths trained

his flashlight down into the quarry. Fly was standing beside a small figure lying in the mud that had been churned into thick liquid by the frequent passage of animals.

"Oh no!" Ivor swore. "Go and tell them, Gwyn. And get your mother to call the ambulance."

But the pathetic sight had launched Gwyn into a violent trembling that almost immobilized him.

"For God's sake, boy. Get ahold of yourself." His father grasped his shoulder. "We need help. Tell them to walk down by the road. We can reach him from the lower fields."

Gwyn rallied his legs into a disorderly run that several times sent him crashing to the ground. *It's my fault,* an inner voice muttered to him while his own cried into the forest of swinging lights, "He's been found. Iolo's here!"

"What's that?" called Mr. Lloyd.

"He's been found."

Someone took up the call. Voices sang out and vanished on the wind. "He's been found." "*Rydym ni wedi ffeindio fo.*" "This way!" "*Ffordd hyn!*"

"Go by the road," Gwyn yelled. "He's in the quarry by the river."

Lights and voices began to converge toward the road while Gwyn raced on to the farmhouse.

Betty Lloyd was in the kitchen with his mother. Her face was an angry tearful red. She practically fell upon him when she heard the news. "Where?" she cried.

"In the quarry," Gwyn panted. "They're going down by the road."

"Is he all right?"

"I don't know, Mrs. Lloyd," he said. "We were on the cliff. We couldn't reach him that way. Dad says to call the ambulance, quick."

"Oh my God," Betty sobbed. "It's always one of mine. I've too many, that's the truth!"

Mrs. Griffiths leaped to the phone and gave directions to the ambulance while Betty Lloyd rushed out into the night, letting the wind blast through the open door, rattling windows and sending loose papers flying around the kitchen.

Gwyn had turned to follow her when his mother shouted, "Stay here, Gwyn," as she replaced the receiver.

"I must go, Mom," he told her.

"But there's no need, dear, now that he's been found. You look dreadful. You should be in bed. Look at the time. Eleven o'clock!"

"I've got to go back," he cried savagely and leaped out. The wind slammed the door for him.

He followed Mrs. Lloyd's frantic footsteps down the lane.

Every time he turned a bend, he lost her on another. At his grandmother's gate he stopped, longing to take shelter with her. Her softly lit window sent out welcoming messages, but he tore himself away and trudged on, past Tŷ Llŷr and another inviting light. Mrs. Lloyd's retreating footsteps were drowned now by the hissing of the turbulent stream.

Just before the lane joined the main road, Gwyn turned on to a narrow footbridge that crossed the stream where it tumbled into the river. He went no farther. Beyond the turn, two Land

Rovers were parked, their nearside wheels deep in the roadside ditch. Behind them the blue light of a police car shed a melancholy glow over the dark shrubbery.

Gwyn could see a circle of lights on the bank beside the quarry. Emlyn came stumping away from it and along the muddy path toward him. "He's OK," he yelled when he saw Gwyn.

The relief that flooded through Gwyn was almost like a pain. It drained him. "Really OK?" he asked weakly when Emlyn stood beside him.

"He's alive," Emlyn gasped for air and continued breathlessly, "but they think he's got a concussion and may have broken some bones."

"Oh no!" Gwyn said.

"I'm going home now," Emlyn told him. "Do you want to walk up with me?"

"No," Gwyn said. "I'll wait for Dad."

Emlyn moved off just as an ambulance screeched around the corner and began to come up the rocky lane, its accompanying siren shrieking above the wind. Gwyn left the bridge and stood against a stone wall, whose topmost stones had begun to spill into the river, so that it offered a rather precarious protection from the torrent beyond. Mr. Davis, Tŷ Coch, and two neighbors approached. They began to run and Mr. Davis shouted, "He's down there!" Then, recognizing the ambulance driver as he stepped out of the vehicle, "You'll need the stretcher, Tom. We don't dare move the boy. He's badly injured!"

Gwyn watched the uniformed men move swiftly into the dark with their flashlights and stretcher. Dappled moonlight glimmered on the water beside them. *Perhaps someone had intended Iolo to drown,* Gwyn thought. He could not help imagining how Iolo's body might have bobbed among the waves. For some reason the picture called to mind the small wooden figures that ancient Celts had thrown into their sacred springs, in the hope of a cure. It gave him the beginning of an idea.

"That you, Gwyn Griffiths?" Mr. Davis had seen him. "Better go home now, lad. There's nothing you can do!"

Gwyn did not move and couldn't trust himself to speak.

Mr. Davis peered at him. "Are you all right, Gwyn?"

"Yes," Gwyn mumbled.

Mr. Davis turned away. He had never been a friend and was always suspicious of Gwyn, who had once wounded his son with a spell.

It began to rain. A slow procession of lights pressed through the gale toward the bridge. Gwyn tensed himself against an inward shaking that threatened to overwhelm him. *My fault,* he thought. *Always, my fault! It always turns against me, my nature. Always getting people lost!* He stood back as they passed him. Iolo's face looked deathly white against the dark blankets on the stretcher; he was making faint sounds like a small wounded animal. Mr. Griffiths brought up the rear. He saw Gwyn and put an arm around his shoulder. "All right, Gwyn. I'll be with you in a minute."

They lifted Iolo into the ambulance, and Mrs. Lloyd climbed in beside him. The doors closed and they tore away into the night.

Police and farmers murmured in groups beside the parked

vehicles. They couldn't fathom why Iolo had come to be in that lonely field, or how he had fallen into the quarry. There were three strands of barbed wire flanking the cliff edge, the lowest strand only a few inches from the ground. The wire was attached, at intervals, to stout fence posts, and Mr. Griffiths checked and repaired the fence every season. Why had Iolo crawled under the wire? He wasn't that sort of boy, Mr. Lloyd had exclaimed. Iolo had never ventured alone beyond the town.

Gwyn, shivering outside the uneasy gathering, couldn't bear the grave and doubtful voices any longer. He backed away then ran up the lane. When he reached his grandmother's gate he flung it open, tore toward the beacon of her window, and tapped on a pane. She was reading by her lamp, looked up when she heard him, saw his face, and ran to open the door.

"What is it, Gwyn?" she asked. "Emlyn was here. He said they'd found Iolo."

He nodded.

"He's all right, then?"

Gwyn began to shake his head from side to side. "Oh Nain," he cried. "Oh Nain, I don't know. I don't know!"

"Stop it, boy. What is it?" She removed his jacket and drew him toward the log fire.

"Nain," he whispered. "It's my fault. I couldn't tell them. What should I do?"

She took his hands. "What have you done, Gwydion Gwyn? Tell me?"

"I asked him to follow Evan Llŷr. I knew it was dangerous

but I did it all the same. The soldier must have pushed him; he meant to kill Iolo, Nain. I know it!"

"What nonsense is this!" She flung his hands away and sat in her chair, glaring up at him. "Wicked, silly boy!"

"Listen," he begged. "Iolo phoned me at six o'clock. He told me Evan had just gone out and he was going to follow him. But the soldier knew. He tricked him, led him along that cliff and . . . and . . ."

"Stop it!" Nain commanded. "You're not rational, Gwydion Gwyn. You've no proof at all. And why didn't you tell the Lloyds about this phone call?"

"I don't know," he said mournfully. He could feel her cold disdain and shuffled away from it to stare into the flames. "What should I do?" he asked.

"You're coming with me," she said, slipping into a black raincoat that lay ready on a chair. "And you're going to tell them everything."

They left her house and walked up to Tŷ Bryn without speaking a word to each other, but on the farmhouse porch Nain peered closely into Gwyn's face and asked, "Why did you tell that poor child to follow Evan?"

Gwyn seemed to find courage in that question. He remembered his anger with Evan, or whatever Evan was, and declared, "He's a devil! I'll prove it to you somehow!"

His grandmother opened the door and prodded him inside. As he removed his boots he could hear the solemn rumble of voices coming from the kitchen. A late-night inquiry was taking place. Gwyn's heart sank.

Nain led him down the hallway, opened the kitchen door, and announced into the crowd of wet and weathered faces, "Gwyn can shed some light on this mystery!"

Gwyn stepped inside and was about to deliver his message when, to his horror, he noticed a tall figure in the shadowy corner beyond the stove.

"What is it, boy?" Mr. Lloyd had swung around in his chair.

"I . . ." Gwyn began. The room was a sea of shapes and faces. He could see nothing distinctly except the dark, utterly motionless soldier. The searching glint of his blue eyes swept through him, seeming to know everything. Instinctively, Gwyn thrust his hand into his pocket and felt for the broken horse. As his fingers closed over it, Evan Llŷr smiled at him.

"Have you got something to say, Gwyn?" his father asked. "What is all this?"

Outside the storm seethed. Every door and window rattled.

Gwyn cleared his throat. "I forgot to tell you," he said lamely. "I'm sorry. Iolo called me and said he was going out. It was six o'clock exactly."

"Why didn't you say so, Gwyn?" Mr. Lloyd sprang out of his chair.

"Called you?" his father bellowed. "What for?"

"Gwyn, how could you forget?" his mother asked.

"I don't know," Gwyn said. "I didn't think it was important — then!"

There were angry protests at this remark but Mr. Lloyd hushed them by saying, "What did my boy say? Why was he going out? And why call you, Gwyn?"

The soldier moved at last. He took one pace forward. The slight smile never left his face. *He is mocking me,* Gwyn thought. *Daring me to accuse him.*

Gwyn accepted the challenge and said loud and very clear, "He said he was going to follow Major Llŷr. I asked him to, you see."

"It was a silly game," his grandmother said quickly.

Was it Gwyn's imagination or was there a slight shifting of blame? Now they were looking at Evan. The soldier stepped boldly into the light and told them, "It was someone else the boy followed, not me!" But his extraordinary storybook appearance seemed to deny this statement. How could anyone in the world be mistaken for such a strange and colorful figure?

Iestyn looked at the soldier, his doubtful black eyes narrowed, and he asked, "Who then?"

"Ask the boy," Evan replied, and although his mouth curved into a smile, the look he shot at Iestyn had ice in it.

"I will," the butcher mumbled and almost ducked away from Evan's deadly stare. The whole room seemed to sway uneasily around the arrogant, unnatural man.

"We better get going, man! It's midnight!" someone said.

The kitchen began to empty. Shoulder to shoulder, friends shuffled to the front door, retrieved their boots from the pile, and pulled on their wet jackets. Outside they called sympathetic messages to Iestyn through the wind. Iolo's father, hunched against the weather, made for his van without a backward glance at Evan.

Evan Llŷr was the last to leave. "*Nos da, teulu Griffiths,*" he said. "Good night, Griffiths family."

Gwyn remained on the porch while his family retreated to the kitchen. There was something odd about Evan's departure.

"He hasn't forgotten his Welsh," said Nain, who had claimed the armchair by the stove.

"Thought he didn't know the language," Ivor said suspiciously.

"Oh, I am sure he did," his wife put in. "Little things, you know!"

"His car wasn't there!" Gwyn said abruptly. "How did he get here without a car? How will he get home?"

"He probably left it at the bottom of the lane," his grandmother retorted. "And you ought to be in bed!" she added tersely.

"I'm going," Gwyn said. *I've turned the tide a bit tonight,* he thought. *I've put them on their guard.*

In his room, he flung himself back on the bed and immediately thought of Iolo wrapped in pale hospital sheets. But he was so exhausted that the fears that had held him awake for so many hours during the past few nights began to fall away from him. To a tiny glow circling the bedpost, he murmured drowsily, "There's work to come, Arianwen. I have to stop the mad prince soon, or else . . ." He fell asleep trying to dream of a solution.

❊ ❊ ❊

The following day they heard that Iolo would recover. He had suffered two fractured ribs, a broken arm and leg, and a nasty head wound. But his limbs would mend and his concussion had not lasted long enough to cause permanent damage. There was one disappointment. He could remember nothing of the incidents that led to his accident. *He's afraid to remember,* Gwyn thought.

That evening he went to see Emlyn. He found his cousin where he expected, in the barn that Idris Llewelyn had converted especially for his son. It was where Emlyn could happily indulge his passion for woodcarving without damaging the neat and polished interior of Tŷ Llŷr.

Once inside the barn Gwyn slid the bolt across the big oak door.

Emlyn grinned. "What's that for?" he asked without taking his eyes off the block of wood before him. He already knew of Gwyn's suspicions. If he found them hard to take, he never showed it.

"I don't want anyone to know about this!" Gwyn said.

"Know about what?" Emlyn slid a chisel carefully along the side of the wood. As he approached, Gwyn could see that something was taking shape there under Emlyn's hands. He walked around his cousin and the tall three-legged table that supported his work, and to his surprise, saw a head that he recognized. The lines were still rough, and the eyes not yet defined, but there was no mistaking the long coiled horn.

"You're making another unicorn!" Gwyn exclaimed.

"He'll rise again, like the phoenix, as brave and bold as before. He's Caradog, the unbowed Celt. And if they defile him, I'll create another and another and another. There'll always be a magical welcome in Pendewi!" Emlyn's speech had always been flamboyant. It came from being born in France, Gwyn had decided.

"I came to ask a favor," he began.

"Fire away," Emlyn said.

Gwyn hesitated. "Hope you won't laugh but I want you to carve a soldier for me. You know, as they are today, in uniform. A helmet, a camouflage jacket, and boots. Not too big." He held his hands six inches apart. "It's for, well, a trick." *That wouldn't do,* he thought. Emlyn deserved better. "No, some witchcraft," he confessed. "Of the healing kind."

Emlyn appeared to accept this as a perfectly normal request. "Do you want me to paint it?" he asked.

This hadn't occurred to Gwyn. "Yes," he said. "Thanks!"

"I'll enjoy it," Emlyn told him. "Copper streaks an' all."

"Gosh, Emlyn. I'm glad you're around." Gwyn drew up a stool beside the unformed unicorn and sat down. "When can you finish it?"

"I've got some seasoned chestnut wood," Emlyn said. "It's used for making toys. Do you remember, Dad had to lop a branch off that old tree up the lane a couple of years ago. It'll take me two or three evenings."

"It'll be another chestnut soldier." Gwyn found himself laughing with a desperate kind of relief.

The door shook and Emlyn's brother, Geraint, called plaintively through it, "Emlyn, Dad wants you!"

"I'll be there in a minute," Emlyn shouted. He lowered his voice. "Gwyn, I know what you're up to. But this kind of thing has to be done gently. You can't cast him into the depths in anger. You want him cured, not dead."

Gwyn realized, with a shock, that this was perhaps what he

had intended, and even now, if this unlikely remedy did not work, it might come to that. "You're right," he said. "Emlyn, you will be careful, don't . . ."

"It'll be safe enough in here," Emlyn told him. "No one else will know!"

"Thanks!" He unbolted the door and ran past Geraint, who was pressed suspiciously close to the wall of the barn. "So long, Geraint!" Gwyn yelled to him.

Confidence surged through him, propelling him into a jaunty downhill sprint to nowhere in particular. He was whistling merrily when he turned on to the bridge where, the previous night, events had reduced him to a wreck. He recalled that sniveling, incoherent self with something like contempt. He was returning to the quarry to prove, somehow, to himself that Iolo's fall had been no accident. He didn't know what he expected to find.

The water had dropped considerably. It ran fast but clear. The rocks were visible and the spray that lapped around them was frosty white.

He was walking purposefully toward the quarry when he saw a fisherman stepping through the water, stealthily, a furled rod in his hand, a basket hung, slantwise, across his back.

It wasn't too late to run away, Evan hadn't seen him, but Gwyn lingered, fascinated by the man's sure movements against the current and the elegant swing of his arm as he cast his line over a deep pool. A silver flash indicated the belly of a salmon as it leaped to catch the fly. Evan began to wind in his line slowly. A battle ensued as the fish thrashed through the spray, desperately unwilling to lose its life. It was a war of wills, as well as strength, lasting several minutes. But the fisherman held steady, playing the line with incredible skill as he edged his way toward the bank. At last he had the writhing fish in his hands. He held it on the stones, dashed a rock against its head and when the fish lay still, deftly removed the hook. He showed no surprise when he saw Gwyn. "*Noswaith dda,*" he greeted him. "Good evening, Gwydion Gwyn!"

He's using the language like a true Welshman, Gwyn thought wryly. *And how does he know my other name?* "*Noswaith dda,*" he returned. "You're catching salmon out of season, Major Llŷr. It's against the law!"

"Are you going to tell on me, then?" Evan asked. He curled the fish into his basket and walked toward Gwyn. "How will they punish me?"

"I won't tell them," Gwyn said, standing his ground. If they were to have a conversation, he might discover what kind of man would be left should the healing spell prove effective.

"*Sut mae'r teulu?*" Evan asked. "How is the family after that long night?"

"*Da iawn, diolch,*" Gwyn replied. "Very well, thank you!"

They began to stroll upriver until they found themselves on a beach of wet stones where the brittle reeds had parted around a huge slab of shale. They shared this seat and began to talk about the moods of the river, the mountains and clouds, mentioning, as they talked, the myths that seemed to have been born out of such a landscape. They spoke in Welsh, the only language that was appropriate for such a discussion. And all the time Gwyn kept thinking, *We're so calm! Is it always like this before a battle?*

It was dusk when they walked together toward Nain Griffiths's house. Evan had promised her a fish for dinner.

When they passed by the still splendid chestnut tree, Evan gazed up at the topmost branches and murmured, "My brother died of that tree."

Gwyn asked, "Were you there?"

"I was standing where you are now," Evan told him, "watching every move my brother made, so that I could remember and repeat his route. He looked down, so triumphant, lost his footing and fell. I thought he was diving into my soul."

They silently regarded the tree, and Gwyn sensed that, for Evan, the moment was critical. He was absorbed in the shape and color of leaves and branches as though he were committing them to memory for a journey he would make, after which all things would have changed beyond his recognition.

In all the world, Gwyn thought, *there can't be a man as lonely as he is!*

They continued their walk without exchanging another word, but when Evan reached Rhiannon Griffiths's white gate, he held out his hand and said, "*Nos da,* Gwydion Gwyn. Thank you for your company!"

Gwyn took the soldier's hand. "*Nos da,*" he said. It seemed like saying good-bye.

CHAPTER NINE

Fire

THE LLOYDS LIVED UNEASILY AFTER IOLO'S ACCIDENT. THEY seemed unable to talk to one another in the comfortable way they had been used to. Mr. Lloyd held opinions he was too afraid to voice, as though once uttered, they would divide him even further from his wife and daughters.

Every day Mrs. Lloyd would visit the hospital and stay an hour with Iolo. Sometimes her husband would accompany her, sometimes she would take one or two of the other children after school.

On the fourth day, Nia begged to go with her parents. She had always disliked hospitals and prepared herself the way she did for a horror movie, expecting a mummylike figure strung up with wires and surrounded with bottles of plasma. She arrived outside the ward clinging to her mother's hand, handkerchief ready, tense and jumpy.

"Calm down, Nia," her father said, his nerves already jangling. "We don't want to upset Iolo!"

"Perhaps you'd better stay outside," Mrs. Lloyd suggested. "I don't think this was a good idea!"

"I'll be calm. I'll be calm, I promise!" Nia assured them breathlessly.

"Well, just step out of the room if you feel bad," her mother said.

They went in.

In many ways it was not nearly as horrific as Nia had expected. There were no bottles of blood in sight, and Iolo was not swaddled in white. A narrow bandage encircled his head like a tiny crown. But his fractured ribs were safely concealed beneath pajamas, and a hump in the bed was the only indication of his injured leg. He was even smiling. But as soon as Nia had taken in all these reassuring signs of recovery, she was immediately alerted by the expression behind that cautious smile. Iolo was frightened. Terrible memories were chasing through his head, and his eyes betrayed him. Like Nia and Bethan, Iolo had inherited his father's dark coloring. His anxious umber-colored eyes strained out of the small sallow face, dense with unrecounted nightmares.

"He's still a bit — distressed," a genial nurse explained. "Perhaps his sister will cheer him up!"

But Nia could do no such thing. She was too shocked by her brother's helpless fear.

Mrs. Lloyd took Iolo's hand. "Have you been eating, dear? Do you like the food better now?"

"You'll be home soon," Mr. Lloyd said with forced heartiness, and unmindful of the alarm that flickered across Iolo's face, added, "We'll have a special meal, all your favorites, won't we, Mom? Roast lamb and mashed potatoes, and apple crumble, you'll like that, won't you?"

Iolo nodded weakly and Nia suddenly realized her brother was being primed for other, more important questions.

"Have you remembered yet, why you were on that cliff? No?" Iolo shrank against the sheets but his determined father lumbered on. "Gwyn Griffiths has told us it was a game and that you phoned him!"

"Leave it, Iestyn," Mrs. Lloyd warned softly. "It's not the time!"

Her husband was unable to do this. Someone was responsible for his son's sorry condition. He had waited long enough. The mystery was tormenting him. "Gwyn says you were following Evan . . ."

"No!" Iolo cried, jerking himself away from the pillows. "I wasn't following anyone. It was a game, see, but the spirits played a trick on me!"

"Spirits? What spirits, dear?" Mrs. Lloyd attempted to touch him but he ducked away from her.

"Evil spirits, Mom," Iolo said gravely. "I know because I could feel them!"

"Feel them?" his parents repeated in alarmed unison.

"Yes," he lowered his voice to share the next secret, "and I saw one, shining!"

"Shining?" said Nia, her mind racing. What had Gwyn been up to? Why had he chosen Iolo for this mission and not her?

"Here," Iolo told her, touching his wrist, "something shining, and here." He pointed to his shoulder.

Iestyn, still bent on a different answer, quietly pressed, "Are you sure, Iolo, that it wasn't your cousin Evan?"

"No! No! No!" Iolo cried, drawing the white sheet up to his face. "It wasn't anyone real, it wasn't!"

A nurse materialized through a distant door as Mrs. Lloyd exclaimed, "How could you, Iestyn? He's not ready." Again she tried to touch her son, and again he resisted her.

"We've got to get to the bottom of this," Iestyn argued.

Nia couldn't bear her favorite brother's confused and troubled stare. Unable to comfort him, she turned away from the scene and began to run, passing the nurse whose stride had quickened into an anxious jog.

Nia slipped through the swinging door and raced down a long, cool passage of numbered and mysterious doors. She didn't stop until she was out in the air. She crossed the parking lot and flopped down on a low brick wall beside the butcher's van. Why was her father, all at once, intent on proving Evan a villain? *Gwyn doesn't trust me,* she thought resentfully, *because I've defended Evan.*

When her parents emerged, they were still arguing and they didn't stop on the way home. Nia had never heard them so angry with each other. Their quarrel alienated her from both of them, making her feel helpless and unhappy.

The atmosphere that waited in number six was no better: Bethan creating a storm of tears in Catrin's arms, Nerys complaining of the noise. Gareth and Siôn had been fighting; Siôn sported a black eye, and Gareth, in an attempt to comfort himself, had reached for the special cookies and knocked a precious glass duck onto the tiled floor, where it still lay in glittering fragments. Alun had locked himself in the bedroom and was shouting, to anyone who cared to listen, that he wasn't "going to open the door until people grew up!"

Betty Lloyd, unable to console her tearful baby, declared that the whole family had gone crazy. "Can't you stop fighting?" she appealed to them. "What's happening to us?"

"It would never have happened except for that Gwyn Griffiths," grumbled Iestyn. "Trouble always follows him. Clings to him like a shadow, it does!"

"It's not his fault," said Nerys. "It's his grandmother, giving him strange ideas. You know what she's like, all those silly stories."

"They're both crazy, then," her father muttered.

"How could you?" Betty cried at her husband's retreating back.

He stomped into his shop just as the front door slammed, and Catrin said, almost to herself, "That's Evan!"

They listened to soft footfalls on the stairs. He never marched or thumped as Nia imagined a soldier used to wearing boots would do. Evan's strides were light and almost musical, like an animal in the forest.

"Evan doesn't like crying babies," Nia remarked, in an attempt to explain his avoidance of the kitchen.

"He doesn't like babies at all," Nerys said as though she sympathized with his point of view. She had tied a pink scarf in a bow on top of her head and was wearing a very un-Nerys blouse with frills all down the front.

"You're just too much at times, Nerys Lloyd!" Catrin cried. "And who said you could borrow my scarf?"

Bethan began to howl again. Catrin left the room, and Nia followed, leaving their mother and Nerys to continue a noisy argument.

What has *happened to us,* Nia wondered. *Something has sneaked into the very heart of our family and it's gnawing away like a treacherous rat.* She wished she was out of it all, up at Tŷ Llŷr with the Llewelyns, where everything was safe and calm and beautiful. Where Idris would laugh her out of her fears, and Elinor would be singing in the garden. But she knew she was needed here. Any little crack in the family might cause it to break apart completely.

She started up to the top floor of the house but remained on the small landing between her room and her parents'. She was aware that she was spying but was past caring now. In fact she realized that she was quite likely to develop this unpleasant trait of hers further; recent events did partly justify a lurking, furtive Nia.

A few seconds after Catrin's door had closed, it opened again just as Nia had expected. She heard her sister cross the hallway and knock on Evan's door.

Tap! Tap! Tap! Very gentle. No answer.

"Evan, are you there?"

A door opened. Two sets of footfalls on the passage, down the stairs, across the hall. The front door opened and closed.

For a brief moment Nia hesitated. Perhaps she thought of Iolo's near-fatal journey, but curiosity eventually sent her bounding down the stairs and out in the street.

They were strolling toward the bridge, Evan's exotic hair unmistakable among the few late shoppers.

She tried to keep up without being seen, but it was impossible. Catrin kept stopping to look into shop windows. It soon became apparent why she was doing this. On the other side of the street, Michael McGoohan was walking arm in arm with Lluned Price. *So what does everyone think about* that? Nia wondered. Michael smiled at her. She smiled back, feeling guilty somehow, at having a foot in both camps. None of it was Michael's fault anyway. When she looked back up the street Catrin and Evan had vanished.

"Darn!" Nia muttered, and a voice behind her asked, "What's the problem?"

She turned to see Gwyn grinning at her. "What're you doing here?" she asked ungraciously.

"Nothing! I'm innocent!" He held up his hands in mock surrender. "I came down with Dad to get some chicken feed."

"We've just been to see Iolo!" she told him.

A shadow fell across his face, changing his confident grin into an anxious line. "How is he?" he asked.

"He's mending physically!" She repeated a nurse's description, "But he's not too good up here!" She touched her head. "And I don't mean crazy; he's frightened, so frightened he can't even bear for our mom to touch him!"

"I'm sorry," Gwyn said and then added, too casually, "He's forgotten, I suppose, what happened?"

"Not exactly." She watched Gwyn's face for signs that might

give him away. "He says a spirit pushed him. Its arm was shining." Gwyn seemed to find this description very promising. "Dad says you told Iolo to follow Evan. Why did you do that? Why didn't you tell me? It's horrible at home. Everyone's angry and hating one another, and none of us really knows why!"

"Look!" Gwyn broke into her angry flow. "It's going to be all right, Nia!"

"What is? What have you done now?" Out of the corner of her eye she saw Mr. Griffiths emerging from Alwyn Farmers, where they sold everything from chicken feed to boots. "I wish you would leave people alone," she added.

"Gwyn!" Mr. Griffiths bellowed from across the street.

"It's too late for that," Gwyn said grimly. He turned his back on her and crossed the road, waving his hand. She couldn't tell if he was feeling the air for rain or had flung a spell into it, for tiny drops of water began to tickle her face.

She ran toward the bridge, regretting her effort at spying. She was too old. Gwyn could enjoy his childish games, but they always seemed to bring bad luck. She decided to take a pondering sort of walk beside the river; the rain would soothe her nerves, and in this way perhaps, she would find a solution to the trouble at home.

After crossing the bridge, Nia took a narrow path that wound between bushes and brambles until it reached the river. The water was very low. She hopped along the beach from rock to stone while the rain beat a companionable rhythm on the water beside her. There was no one in sight. Beyond the reach of all the worry and grimness she began to sing chirpily, "Who cares, anyway? Who cares?" She found herself wading through a forest of reeds, and crouching down among the thick stems, it occurred to her that she was in an excellent position for a spy. The thought was hardly formed when she realized that it was exactly what she was.

On the other side of the river where the bank rose house-high, beyond the beach, two figures were clambering down. They stood a moment on the narrow strip of pebbles, enjoying the shower. Evan's hair was all black now, it drooped about his head like a slippery helmet. Catrin's sweater clung tight as skin, and her hair hung in long coils almost to her waist.

Unseen, Nia froze. She watched, as she might have watched an illustration to a fairy tale, waiting for the picture to spring to life, yet dreading it. And when it did she observed every detail, preserving it somewhere in her mind as something that happened outside her life, to creatures in a story that she didn't know at all. For Evan's kiss was not gentle. Like dreadful sorcery it turned Catrin to stone, and for a moment, all the fairy tales turned backward as in an ugly mirror. The prince didn't waken this sleeping beauty, he sent her scrambling away from him, up the narrow path, all mud and tears.

Nia, wishing she was a hundred miles away, could only focus on the prince as he paced the rainy beach, roaring with terrible laughter. And then, as he slipped down onto the stones until he was almost lying in the water, his laughter gave way to the howl she'd heard before, a dreadful sound that sank deep into her and made her sob against her hand, "It isn't him. It isn't him at all!" Catrin had seen the terrible brimstone eyes, she'd seen the monster and been kissed by him. At that moment Nia hated Evan, not for hurting Catrin but for kissing her.

Soon the only sound was the rain. Nia grew stiff with waiting. Her eyes ached with watching the solitary form beside the water. She couldn't move, for his gaze seemed to bore straight through the reeds that concealed her. She became convinced that he could see her, but at last he stood up wearily and began to walk upriver. She watched him slowly recede into the curtain of rain, stumbling through the pools but still tall and straight, welcoming the weather as a sort of sanctuary. When she lost all sight of him she ran home, slipped upstairs, and managed to change out of her wet clothes before anyone saw her.

Evan didn't appear for supper. Catrin's eyes were red and she had dried her hair carelessly into what looked like a great mound of yellow cotton candy. Her wild appearance caused Nerys to remark, "Good grief, Cat, you look as though you've been ravaged by hounds!"

Catrin leaped up with a screech and made for the door, shouting, "Shut up! Shut up! Shut up!" to all the walls and furniture, before she ran out.

Mrs. Lloyd frowned reprovingly at Nerys. "Why can't you be more sensitive?" she sighed.

"I am sensitive," Nerys returned, "only none of you realize it. You all think *she's* the only sensitive one because she fits the picture of a talented and temperamental person. Well, I've got feelings, too. But no one tells *me*, 'How pretty you are!' 'How lovely your hair looks today!' You don't even notice what I'm wearing."

This uncharacteristic outburst stunned Betty Lloyd, who began to look at her oldest daughter with dawning sympathy, but Iestyn, refusing to believe his daughter's moods had anything to do with growing up, said, "You're all working too hard. Exams for this, exams for that, music as well!"

No one argued with him.

At eight o'clock the big oak dresser gave a little shudder while Nia and Nerys were washing up. A drawer fell out and cutlery jangled onto the tiles like an eerie percussion. At half past eight, a glass rolled off the bathroom shelf. Ten minutes later, the bookcase in the hall emptied itself. It did this in a helpless desultory way, dripping books onto the floor one by one, as though it was trying to disguise its tipsiness. "This house is crooked," Alun complained as he attempted to stem the flow of ancient weighty tomes.

At nine o'clock the television trembled into silence, the newscaster glowed brilliant pink then vanished and a blank screen seemed to advise that bed was the only answer. Then the lights went out. A power cut, they thought, to wind up their unhappy day. They all took candles and went upstairs in a defeated weary way, longing for sleep but, somehow, not expecting it. The rain became a steady downpour, beating through their dreams.

It was past midnight when the knocking began. Except for Bethan, the household was awake but they seemed to think that if they didn't acknowledge the noise, it would disappear.

It grew louder. Nia sat up. The room was shaking now. The

temperature had risen by twenty degrees at least. Sweat trickled down her back. Downstairs a deafening crash sent the family tottering to their doors, calling to one another, "What's that? Mom, Dad, what is it?"

Mr. Lloyd, candle in hand, went down to the kitchen. "Goodness, it's the dresser," he exclaimed. "Smashed the table, right through. We can't do anything about it now." Something roared above him, the ceiling cracked and flung hot plaster through the air. He leaped out of the kitchen crying, "It's a quake!"

The Lloyds clattered downstairs and huddled together in the living room, blessing the day they had decided to bring the oil lamps from Tŷ Llŷr. They sat very close to one another, Bethan clinging to her mother, too afraid to cry; the girls holding hands, tense against the sudden jerks that followed the thunder.

"It's so hot," Alun remarked in a whisper. "Like there's a fire in the cellar."

"Is it the end of the world?" Siôn asked.

"No, No! It's a disturbance, that's what it is," their father reassured them. But he sounded too confident. "Weather patterns all gone wrong. It'll sort itself out," he added emphatically.

Nia bravely joined Gareth by the window. The streetlights were out, and there wasn't a flame or a glow to be seen in any of the neighbors' windows. Perhaps they were sleeping through the storm. Hail began to tap against the panes; for a few seconds each tiny stone glowed red as though it was an ember from some monstrous bonfire in the sky.

Nia and Gareth stepped back while, behind them, their

family gasped, "It's impossible, it can't be! What's happening now?" And then a groan descended through the storm, hardly distinguishable as human. They all knew where it came from but no one mentioned it.

He's alone, Nia thought, *but they're pretending he doesn't exist. They don't want him in here with them.*

She took her candle from the sideboard and went to the door.

"Where are you going, dear?" her mother whispered.

"I'm tired," Nia replied. "I'm going to bed."

"Careful on the stairs," her father advised.

Before anyone could decide to follow her, Nia slipped out and closed the door. She slowly mounted the stairs while the candle flared in sudden drafts that rearranged the neat shadow creeping behind her. There were sounds in the house that she could not identify: rustling, hissing noises that might have been raindrops, but when she tried to picture them, she could only imagine little buds of flame sprouting through the walls. Try as she might she couldn't calm the shaking hand that held her candle in its holder. On the landing the sounds intensified, they rippled toward her down the narrow corridor like amplified waves in a tunnel. She longed to let the tide drive her away, but instead clung to the banister for a moment and then set off to the room that held that secret fire.

It seemed like such a long journey. So many times she might have turned back, but each time she felt a quiet and desperate call tugging at her, and pressed on. At the end of the corridor she put a hand on Evan's door. It almost burned her. Nia, who believed in ghosts and magic, did not believe that disturbing weather patterns had caused this terrible heat. Nightmares had overflowed into their home.

She opened the door and stepped into a room that sweltered like a melting pot. Colors flared across the walls: scarlet, orange, green, too bright to look at. They sang and crackled in a shining circle — tormenting little flames that threatened to break into the room, greedy for life. Nia stood on the threshold, petrified, telling herself that nothing was real except the man surrounded by his dreams.

Evan was lying on the floor. Whether he had fallen there or had chosen this position she couldn't tell. His head was turned toward the curtained window, and his eyes were closed. His face glistened with sweat.

Nia tiptoed carefully around the tall, prone figure, drew the curtains and flung open the window. A wonderfully cold breeze rushed past her, breathing reality into the room. For a moment the flames brightened, angrily fighting back, and then they died. Evan stirred and gave a low moan but he didn't wake. Nia set the candle on the floor and, kneeling beside him, gently touched his damp head.

"Please help this poor soldier," she implored the cool night air. "His dreams are burning him up!"

CHAPTER TEN

The Wizard and the Wand

NIA TOLD NO ONE THAT SHE'D SEEN THE EPICENTER OF THEIR fiery storm. She left Evan still sleeping, but more peaceful. She liked to think that she had coaxed a calm spirit into the room. The thunder gradually receded and a cool nocturnal breeze roamed through the house, comforting the Lloyds into a few hours of sleep.

When Nia went downstairs the next morning she found that Evan had left the house. He had gone even before Mrs. Lloyd made her way to the kitchen to figure out how she could make breakfast in a room full of broken china. Confronting her, the huge oak dresser lay at a treacherous angle across the broken table, blocking the light, daring the family to touch it.

"I'll ring Morgan the Smithy and we'll have it fixed in no time," Iestyn said with forced cheerfulness.

Morgan, proud of his strength, was always ready to oblige. "Good heavens!" he said when he saw the chaos. "Have your lads done this?"

"It was an earthquake," Iestyn told him gravely.

"Never," said Morgan winking at the boys. "There was a bad

storm, but no quake, Iestyn. What were you drinking last night?"

The family didn't laugh.

They soon learned that although their neighbors had suffered a power failure, none of them had noticed a rise in temperature or seen glittering hailstones in the sky; they hadn't even had their houses rocked.

"I don't think they believe us," Mrs. Lloyd complained. "They still think we're superstitious mountain people!" She phoned the Griffiths's farmhouse where she knew she'd always find sympathy.

Gwyn heard the news just before he left for school and wondered if he was responsible. The previous evening he had collected a small carved soldier from Emlyn. He had taken it high onto the mountain, where shining clear water sprang from the rocks, filling a dark, ice-cold pool. Gwyn had thrown his wooden soldier into the center of the pool, watched it vanish and chanted a tranquil poem across the water. Widening concentric ripples spilled toward him and he had begged the spirit of the pool to forgive and heal Evan Llŷr. He had waited in vain for the light wood to surface but the water had swallowed it up. He had thought it was a good sign at first, that the spring water had taken the soldier to its heart and would cure him. But as he had walked home the clouds had felt leaden and wrathful about him, threatening to disgorge something far worse than rain onto his bare head.

So he was not entirely surprised to hear Alun's unsure voice recount the night's disturbance. Gradually Gwyn learned of the shaking walls, the rain of hailstones, and the inexplicable smell of burning that had crept through number six.

"I only made him angry, then," Gwyn muttered.

"What've you done?" Alun asked, not really believing his friend could have been responsible for such amazing events. He knew Gwyn had a power he didn't understand, but he disliked the supernatural.

Gwyn hesitated to burden Alun further. "I can't explain now," he said. "I'll pop in after school." He was eager to discover, for himself, any trace of the extraordinary fire that Evan had, without a doubt, drawn around him.

It was far worse than he'd imagined. The house was possessed by a quiet chaos. Alun's mother sat beside the broken table while her husband wearily hammered and plastered. Mrs. Lloyd mumbled about hallucinations. It was like a giant had crashed through her house, she said, tipping furniture, breathing filthy smoke into the rooms.

Embarrassed by their mother's temporary madness, the children foraged for bread and snacks. Nerys made tea and tried to cheer her mother, while Catrin withdrew to share her troubles with the piano. Tragic and unfamiliar music began to penetrate the house, even following Alun, Gwyn, and Nia to the very top floor, where they had retreated to discuss the night's events.

They sat side by side on Nia's bed, staring at Iolo's reproachful empty one, while Gwyn described his attempt to rid Evan of the dreadful prince he harbored.

Alun's face was a mixture of distaste and alarm. He might have dismissed his sister's stories, but he couldn't argue with his friend. "You really believe in this demon, don't you?" he said glumly.

"I know it almost as well as I'd know a friend, now," Gwyn told him. "And I honestly thought I'd help Evan to fight it. But it's stronger than I dreamed!"

"And the fire in our house was his nightmare, wasn't it?" Nia said, peering at him.

"It was real," Alun insisted.

They both turned to Gwyn for confirmation. "Nia's right," he said. "But — which nightmare? How can we know if he was dreaming of the fire that burned his friends or that other one nearly two thousand years ago."

"Oh no," Alun groaned. "How can you have someone else's dream?"

"When you're possessed," Gwyn told him fiercely.

Nia still kept the secret flames to herself. They belonged only to him, she thought. She had trespassed and shared his nightmare. Nain Griffiths had told her she would be the one to find a happy ending.

Alun kicked the bedpost, hating the inexplicable. "OK," he said at last. "Suppose it's true what you say and Evan is — possessed by an old Celtic prince, suppose he's reliving terrible memories, trying to murder Iolo, stealing Catrin, burning our house — what are we going to do about it?"

A crash from below diverted Gwyn from answering. They leaped to the door and ran down the first flight of stairs, expecting more of the same sounds to follow. But on the landing Gwyn held up his hand, warning them not to approach the second flight. The melancholy piano had stopped but the ensuing silence was somehow even more menacing.

Peering cautiously over the banister they saw Evan standing in the hall. He wore a huge scarf around his shoulders, deep crimson striped with gold, and a brooch glittered on his chest. There were rings on his hands and a gold band peeped from the edge of his sleeve. He had flung open the front door so violently that it had crashed back too far, fracturing the wooden frame. The window in the door, too, had cracked and slivers of glass suddenly fell onto the floor with muted little tinkles.

Iestyn emerged from the kitchen. He sidled past Evan, who neither moved nor greeted him. The butcher felt the splintered wood and closed the door, nervously murmuring, "It can't be fixed. I'll see to it later!"

Mrs. Lloyd came into the hall. She stared at Evan, and the broken door window, rubbed her mouth with her knuckle, and asked, "Evan are you — all right?"

A fearful sound came from him, an even deeper voice than the one they knew. Betty Lloyd cringed away from it, moved around him, and bending almost double, knelt to pick up the broken glass. Evan strode farther into the hall and turned to watch her as Catrin appeared in the doorway of the front room.

Mother and daughter looked at each other and then at Evan. He kicked a fragment of glass toward the kneeling woman and crunched his heel upon another.

"It's not him," Nia croaked in a desperate whisper. "It's not Evan."

He looked up at that and hurled an oath at them.

"Who is snooping on the stairs?" he roared.

Alun, Nia, and Gwyn pelted back to the top floor of the house. They stood on the narrow landing, searching one another's faces in the gloom, and Alun, all at once believing everything, said, "What should we do now?"

"Something impossible," Gwyn told him.

Nia stared hard at Gwyn, trying to guess what he might have to do, but she realized that Gwyn himself was not entirely clear about what it was.

After a moment of silence she went down to help her mother with the broken glass. Music came from the room beside them and when she asked where Evan had gone, Mrs. Lloyd directed a quick frown at the closed living room door.

They're together, Nia thought. *Has Catrin recovered from the monster's kiss, or has he captured her at last?*

The front door creaked open again and Gwyn's father thrust his head inside. "Was this the storm then?" He nodded at the cracks that threatened to set the door free.

"Indeed it was," Mrs. Lloyd said, carefully avoiding her daughter's gaping stare. But Nia had no intention of telling the truth.

"He's here, then?" Mr. Griffiths looked up the stairs to where Gwyn and Alun had appeared. "Thought he would be!"

"Will you have a cup of tea now, Ivor?" Betty Lloyd asked a little unwillingly.

"Do you need some help, Betty? You look real shaken up." She shook her head. "Morgan came around this morning."

"We'd best be off, then. There's a lot to do."

She knew, of course. She'd been a farmer's wife and was

beginning to wish she was back there, safe on the mountain, where there were no ghosts to trouble her children and shake her house.

Gwyn winked at Nia as he passed her. He hoped he wore a confident look but doubted it. She smiled bleakly at him and said, "See you at school."

Mr. Griffiths closed the door on harassed number six and climbed into the Land Rover after Gwyn.

"Did quite a bit of damage then, that storm," he remarked as they drove past a broken gutter.

"Yes, a lot," Gwyn agreed.

❊ ❊ ❊

Mrs. Griffiths was visiting her mother-in-law when they got home. Father and son helped themselves to tea and slabs of bread and honey before each went to his own work. Mr. Griffiths to his cattle, Gwyn upstairs, ostensibly to do his homework. His room reeked of chemicals. Five hundred sheep had been dipped that week and the pungent smell would hang around the farm for days. Gwyn closed his window but made no attempt to get out his books.

He had to do something very soon, and he needed help. It wasn't enough, this time, to rely on a trickle of energy through his fingers. He had two monsters to face, one reinforcing the other, not fighting it. And he'd been the cause. He'd bound that poor soldier into another story, sent him tumbling into a state of madness where he couldn't forgive or forget the fire that had taken his friends. Gwyn knew what he had to do, of course. He had known for some time but had refused to recognize the directions his own small voice was giving him. It was such a very big step. He needed to think about it.

For a long time he sat watching Arianwen spinning in a corner. She was exceptionally busy today, providing an entrance to the country he would have to visit. Once Nia had slipped into the mysterious time beyond that web, but he'd been nearby to help her back. How would he return, with no one to guide him? He'd have to trust his familiar: a tiny spider that looked quite ordinary in daylight.

Should he have more to eat before he set off? No. Poets and magicians fasted before attempting feats of great magnitude. He brushed his hair for the occasion and emptied his pockets. In case he was delayed, he tore a page from his exercise book and wrote on it: *Gone to see Emlyn about homework. Might stay late!* He took the note to the kitchen and left it on the table propped against the honey jar. Then, noticing the half-moons of grime under his fingernails, he gave his hands a good scrub in the kitchen sink.

When he got back to the attic the web was ready. It hung across an entire corner from ceiling to floor: a huge screen that capriciously mirrored his room in false shapes and colors; his bed had become a frothy green bank, the cupboard had multiplied into a wood of twisted gray trees; the carpet was tufted with wildflowers where a reedlike shadow stood, who must have been Gwyn's own reflection.

He searched the beams for his spider and identified her at last: a tiny glimmer beside the silver pipe. She seemed to indicate that he should take it, so leaping on the bed, he seized the pipe and immediately felt his legs lighten. In a strange, almost airborne fashion he stepped down and walked toward the web. The pipe began to tell him things he did not understand but when he touched the gossamer it began to make sense. "Come forward and bow your head, now your feet!"

Gwyn held his breath. He shut his eyes against the sticky threads, lowered his head, and moved through the web, remembering to call a brief farewell to the spider watching from her perch. When he opened his eyes again he was met with such a blackness he panicked himself into believing he was blind. But the pipe in his hand hummed in such a comforting way that he took a courageous step forward, and finding nothing to stop him, took another and another, until he was moving confidently forward to where a faint light illumined the landscape.

He was in a forest, a vast never-ending sea of trees. He knew it was vast as though he had lived there always. He could feel the endless repetition of branches stretching to the fringes of the land. It was an ancient forest. The slowly brightening dawn light showed him huge, moss-grown trunks, plants that hung from the branches like Christmas decorations, and a deep carpet of undisturbed leaves that smelled indescribably old and earthy. Gwyn became aware that he was following a thin trail where the undergrowth had been brushed with a silvery dew, like the wake of a snail, and he knew that he was not alone.

Creatures crept behind him, accompanying his footfalls with soft breathing and busy scurrying that was not at all alarming. Once Gwyn glimpsed a great stag moving in the shadows, but he was not afraid. He felt every animal to be his friend.

The light became sunshine beaming into a glade where some-one sat motionless on a huge seat, roughly hewn from a single rock that glittered with threads of quartz. The man had his back to Gwyn. He wore a cloak made of strips of fur intertwined with dark feathers whose color shifted through a hundred vari-ations with every breath of air. His hair was shining white and lay in a stiff mane down to his shoulder blades.

The stranger heard Gwyn's approach and turned in his direc-tion. He showed no surprise on seeing a twenty-first-century boy, in fact he seemed to expect him. Gwyn, however, stopped dead in his tracks; he might have been looking at a matured and weathered version of himself. The white-haired man was not old; he had every one of Gwyn's features: the dark eyes and heavy eyebrows, even the Griffiths dent in his chin. He smiled, showing excellent white teeth and said, in perfectly understandable Welsh, "*Croeso*, Gwydion Gwyn! Welcome!" He motioned the boy to sit at his feet, and when Gwyn was comfortable, began to talk as naturally as a parent embarking on a bedtime story.

Gwyn slowly came to realize that he was hearing a story told, not as a legend but as an episode in someone's life, where spells were just as commonplace as cups of tea. Gwydion, the magi-cian, the greatest storyteller in all the world was relating a chapter that had been missed in the writing of the legends. He spoke for a long time, and while Gwyn listened the sun died and a brilliant moon filled the open sky above them. It was the story of two princes, brothers, one kind and gentle, the other willful and strong. They were so close they might have been two sides of one man. But somewhere in their lives the stronger man had swept his gentle brother into his own fierce life, swamped him so that he had no place in the story. And the strong prince loved so passionately, hated so savagely, committed crimes of such wickedness that even when he died, his spirit was stranded outside the Otherworld where all great warriors live, until Gwydion, almost by accident, trapped the violent spirit in an exquisite carving, a small ebony horse that had been a gift from his brother, Gilfaethwy. But when his spell was accomplished, the horse had twisted and screamed itself into such a monstrosity that Gwydion had locked it out of his sight. "And that mad prince was Efnisien, my own nephew," the magician said a little sadly. "He was my sister Penarddun's son."

The storyteller's voice had almost sent Gwyn into a state of dreaming. "I had forgotten he was related," he said, shaking himself into action. He stood and told his ancestor, "Efnisien is free again."

Gwydion said, "Well, boy, I know. Why else would I have told you all this?"

"Forgive me," Gwyn persevered, "but it isn't an answer to my problem."

"A story is an answer," Gwydion replied. "Perhaps you haven't asked the right questions."

"Very well, then. What must I do?"

"Whatever you do, don't do it in anger," Gwydion said gravely. Then all at once he took a long stick of ash wood that lay beside him, spun it three times in the air and let it fall. And where it touched the earth sparks flew out in a brilliant display of shapes and colors: dragons, flowers and butterflies, beasts and birds blazed about Gwyn's head and then slid away in a bright procession through the trees.

Gwyn regarded the wand for a moment, wondering if it was a gift. He could not bring himself to touch it. "Gwydion," he said. "I'm afraid of magic. Everything I do — it always turns on me. My decisions are hopeless. I've made too many mistakes." He looked up at his ancestor, hoping for a word to set him once and for all on the right road for a magician.

But Gwydion said, "I, too!"

"You?"

"We all do!" Gwydion laughed. "My uncle Math turned me into a stag once for misbehaving, and on another occasion a wild sow." He threw back his head and gave a delighted guffaw. "Imagine," he roared, "a sow. I can't tell you what it was like. I found myself relishing — well, you wouldn't believe it!"

"I would," Gwyn said, joining in the laughter. "We've kept pigs."

At this Gwydion's laughter redoubled, and Gwyn fell back on the ground, giggling hysterically. In all his life he had never felt so carefree. If only he'd known that magic did not have to be a burden. "You mean a magician can misjudge?" he asked breathlessly. "Can blunder?"

"Nothing is straightforward," Gwydion replied. "It's like life. But isn't it fun to leap in the dark?"

They smiled at each other in perfect understanding. Friends forever, and Gwyn, at last, felt able to murmur, "Gwydion, I haven't grown for nearly four years."

For a moment he thought his ancestor was going to find another excuse for laughter, but instead he nodded in a thoughtful way. "I'm sure you will," he said. "But is it so important?" And when Gwyn grimaced he added, "You're not blaming your genes, are you? I'm no dwarf! Bear up, boy! Laugh a bit more. Let a chuckle grow inside you until you have to stretch to keep up with it. Now take my ash wand and see what you can make of it."

It was a slim uncomplicated-looking stick, and yet it had released a cloud of magic. When Gwyn picked it up he felt the echo of his touch ringing through the wand like music. He knew he must give something in return for this precious gift and tentatively offered the pipe that Gwydion had sent him four years before.

"I'll keep it safe!" his ancestor said.

A quietness hung between them, and Gwyn was aware that there was still something unfinished about their exchange. There was a meaning to the story that he had missed, and running through it quickly in his mind, what surfaced every time he thought of the broken horse, was a restless sort of anxiety. "Will that tormented prince ever be happy?" he asked. "Can I help him into the Otherworld?"

He was rewarded with a golden smile. "You've already taken the first step," Gwydion said, sliding gracefully from his seat, and without another word he vanished into the black shadows of the forest. Gwyn could not even hear a footfall. And yet when he had curled himself into a sleeping position on the ground, he thought he heard a voice, very close to his ear, whisper, "*Pob hwyl*, Gwydion Gwyn! Good luck!"

When he woke up he was lying on his bed with his mother leaning over him, an expression of irritated concern on her face. "Gwyn, what's the matter with you?" a rather distant voice came grumbling through to him, and then more loudly, "Emlyn's downstairs; he says he hasn't seen you. Why leave that note?"

"Sorry, Mom." He tried to wring a reasonable response out of himself. He felt utterly exhausted. "I meant to go. Must have fallen asleep!"

"Supper's ready!"

He thought he'd spent twenty-four hours in a forest, had it been only one? He swung his legs over the side of the bed, knocking something on to the floor.

"What's that?" Mrs. Griffiths frowned at the stick beside his bed.

He was about to inform her that it was a wand, of course, when his twenty-first-century self caught up with him and he replied, "It's for measuring, Mom."

"Gwyn, Love." She gave him a sympathetic glance at last. "You're not still worried about growing, are you?"

"No," he assured her. "I'm measuring furniture and that, for school. It's a project."

She gave a sigh of relief and left him to tidy himself up.

His legs felt like lead. *I suppose I've walked pretty far,* he told himself, and then he looked in his mirror. It was not Gwyn the boy who returned his puzzled stare, but a full-grown man with white hair and deep lines etched into his parchment-brown skin. It was Gwydion the magician. Yet Gwyn's mother had noticed nothing.

Had he exchanged more than a gift with Gwydion, then? Had unseen age come with the wand, while all his youthful, undisturbed features had been left in the forest, for a middle-aged wizard to enjoy? What a trickster!

"How old am I?" Gwyn asked the mischievous reflection. "Two thousand years or forty?" The wizard wasn't telling. "Will I be thirteen on Sunday? You surely can't take my birthday away from me! Tricks are all very well," he went on, facing the mirror squarely, "but will I be strong enough now to fight the prince, or will I crumble to dust the moment he touches me?"

CHAPTER ELEVEN
An Ancient Magic

WHEN MR. LLOYD HAD REPAIRED THE TABLE WELL ENOUGH TO withstand a meal, the family settled down to a cold supper. Only the twins had an appetite but the others forced themselves through the motions of eating as a way of comforting their mother who seemed more distraught than ever.

Nia couldn't rid her mind of the wild presence that had burned into every corner of their narrow hall. He had shone like the spirit who had tricked Iolo; he had gleamed gold with his glittering bracelet, rings, and jeweled brooch. Had he stepped back through time to retrieve the effects of a warrior prince? Or had madness driven him to buy an exotic costume for the final seduction, the moment when he would carry her sister thousands of years away?

Evan went out after his brief visit and did not return. Catrin left her music looking as though goblin's kisses were burning both her cheeks. No one alluded to the soldier's outlandish appearance. They tried to wish the memory away.

The rain fell steadily through the night. By morning the river had risen more than three feet. The mountains were scribbled with tiny white torrents that gushed down through the rocks and the scree. The ditches swelled and spilled across the narrow roads, making them almost impassable.

Nia caught a glimpse of Gwyn in school; he was dragging himself along the corridor and coughing like a geriatric.

"He's a real wimp, that Gwyn," said Gwyneth Bowen. "Did you see what happened on the playground?"

Nia had not seen. She'd spent her break trying to catch up with homework.

"Fell flat on his face, he did," Gwyneth informed her gleefully, knowing Gwyn was a friend of Nia's. "Just because one of those jets flew over. He was shaking like a leaf. What a laugh!"

"Perhaps he knows something we don't," Nia retorted. "They crash sometimes, don't they?" She had heard the jet, rumbling overhead. It was a familiar sound but she could never help reacting, hunching her shoulders and blocking her ears. She wasn't the only one either. No one, however, had gone as far as flinging themselves to the ground. What had become of Gwyn, just when she needed him most?

Nia caught Gwyn's eye in the lunch line and he gave her a sly half smile. After school he accompanied the Lloyds to number six, but instead of following Alun into the kitchen, he hung back and touched Nia's arm. She waited in the hall while he gasped for breath.

"What is it?" she whispered. "You're like an old man."

"Not old, just out of breath," he replied. "It's household air, I'm not used to it."

"What do you live in then, a forest?"

"You don't realize how funny that is," he said wryly.

"I heard you were diving for cover when the jets flew in today!"

"Took me by surprise. Look, can you come outside, there's a dreadful smell in here!"

"It's only Mom's cooking," Nia said indignantly, and then admitted, "It could be disinfectant, it does stink a little."

He opened the front door and pulled her out on to the pavement. "That's better," he said, breathing in a more normal fashion. "I suppose I look quite ordinary to you."

"I wouldn't say that," she replied. "You've never looked absolutely average and today you're really weird."

"But you'd recognize me?"

"No, I think I'm talking to a buzzard."

He gave a high plaintive "hee-haw" in response and then laughed. He was not someone else and yet he was not quite Gwyn. It was very unnerving to think that this heavy-breathing, rather jokey person was all that she had to rely on. "Gwyn," she said gravely, "are you going to help us?"

He looked up the road, frowned at a passing car and said tantalizingly, "I suppose you're shouting because of all this."

"I'm not shouting!" She had the impression that he was trying to adjust to the atmosphere, as though the world of traffic and conversation was too overwhelming for him to give her the attention she needed.

"Yes," he said at last. "I know what to do, but it'll be up to you, too."

"What do I have to do?" she asked, reluctant to commit herself to any frontline activity.

Having adapted himself to the situation, he became quietly efficient. "Tomorrow's Saturday," he said. "Catrin will be rehearsing at the community center. Tell Evan Llŷr she wants to see him by the bridge. Say it's urgent!"

"But . . ." she said wildly.

"There's no room for dithering, Nia. He'll be there, in your house and you'll all be glad to get rid of him. I'll fix things!"

"When?" she cried, beginning to panic at the deceit she'd have to use.

"At dusk," he told her. "You'll know. Now I've got arrangements to make."

She watched him swaying up the road, wanting to ask him so many questions, yet knowing he'd moved on, somewhere far beyond her little problems. What did he intend to do? Would he harm her cousin? Was there a place on the clock for dusk? Suppose she didn't time her mission properly?

✳ ✳ ✳

Gwyn walked all the way home, surveying his territory, marking footsteps in his mind, judging the swell of the river, and feeling the approaching weather. After a while his feet became accustomed to the hard asphalt. He would have to drag himself a little farther into the present, he realized, to grapple with a soldier whose anger burned in two worlds. He needed a storm — drowning weather.

When he reached his grandmother's cottage he found her in

the garden, piling leaves ready for a bonfire. "Are you coming down tomorrow, then, Gwydion Gwyn?" she asked. "To share my Halloween fire?"

Halloween? He'd forgotten. *How appropriate,* he thought wryly. But there would be no fire. "It'll rain, Nain," he told her, "and I'm sorry, but I'll be busy."

"Rain? Nonsense!" she snorted, and then she looked intently at him, as though something in his attitude had filtered through to her at last. She came to the gate and asked, "How do you know?"

He felt himself give the same smile that his ancestor had passed on to him. "I know," he said lightly.

She peered at him, searched his face with her bird-bright eyes and whispered, "Gwydion Gwyn, have you been back?"

He nodded, still smiling.

"And did you meet . . . ?"

"I did," he told her.

She gave a long happy sigh. "I'm so glad for you, Gwydion Gwyn."

"I'll tell you one thing," he said with the air of someone who was passing on information about a mutual friend. "Gwydion is a rascal. He blunders like I do, and I know that sometimes I shall have to leap into the dark, but Nain" — he was amused by the crooked little expression of gladness that had gradually crept into her face — "I'll never turn from it again. It's not a burden, you see."

"You speak of him in the present," Nain said.

"Do I? Well, he's here, isn't he?" Gwyn spun in the lane, arms akimbo, his hands eventually coming to rest on top of his black hair.

They laughed together in a way they hadn't done for a long time, and Gwyn at last confided, "He's in my reflection, Nain. He's taken me over, he breathes through me, laughs inside my head, and he's not above a bit of wickedness. I'll have to watch that!"

"And has Gwydion shown you how to solve your — problem?" she asked carefully.

"He's given me the means," Gwyn said, "and I know what to do."

"You won't harm the soldier, Gwyn?"

"I told you, I'm leaping in the dark. I'll save the Lloyds, I'll trap the demon, but as for Evan Llŷr, I can't tell!" He was sorry to disappoint her. "Not everyone can win," he said regretfully. "You know that, Nain."

"I know." She gave a disconsolate little shrug and then asked hopefully, "But you'll try, Gwydion Gwyn, won't you, not to cause him any more pain?"

Gwyn couldn't promise that.

Just before she disappeared into her house, Nain called, "It's your birthday, the day after tomorrow. Thirteen is a special age. How shall we celebrate?"

There may be nothing to celebrate, he thought. "Let's wait and see," he said.

He continued up to Tŷ Bryn, wondering if this older man,

this alter ego, would always be with him. He needed Gwydion's strength but what if he never broke free of the quizzical middle-aged reflection, the long, weatherworn fingers, and the forest-dweller's cough. *I'll put my worries aside,* he thought, *as Gwydion would have done — is doing. Because I'm him, or he's me.* He found himself laughing a lot louder than Gwyn Griffiths usually did.

When he reached home he resolved to sleep in the air that night. He would take a blanket out to the open barn where the weather could sing him to sleep. He needed to dream.

A distant rumble heralded the storm he'd predicted.

❋ ❋ ❋

Saturday was a dark day. The sunlight was obscured by a thick blanket that drizzled steadily into the valley. The river swelled to a dangerous torrent and children were forbidden to play on the banks. Nia wondered how she would know dusk from daytime.

The prince returned at noon and joined them for a meal. His tartan scarf had been discarded in favor of a scarlet shirt, pinned at the neck with the same shining brooch. He was a stranger to them now. The stare he leveled at Catrin across the table was quite outrageous, and when she shied away from it, embarrassed and afraid, he gave another of his desperate laughs.

Nerys tried to diffuse the atmosphere by talking of the weather. She'd curled her hair and looked almost pretty. She chattered on, rather wildly for her, until Evan suddenly laid a hand on hers and said with quiet venom, "You talk too much, my dear. Plain girls should always keep quiet!"

Stunned, Nerys's mouth snapped shut. She stared ahead at a

cup on the dresser. A single tear rolled down her cheek. It was, somehow, even more dreadful than Catrin's awkward fear.

And then another laugh descended on them, striking every member of the family a blow from which they couldn't recover. Even the twins were silent. This was the soldier they had wanted, but he terrified them.

At either end of the table, Iestyn and Betty gazed helplessly at each other, wondering how to end the madman's occupation of their home.

My prince has gone, Nia thought. *Vanished, swallowed up by someone else's life.* The window showed a sky of endless gray and she began to worry that her part of the magical proceedings would go wrong. Suppose she called Evan too soon and he returned from an empty bridge, outraged and even more violent.

He spent the rest of the day in their living room, leaving the door open to flaunt his possession of the sofa. His feet were over one arm, his head resting on the other; his eyes were closed, hands clasped across his chest. Now and again he emitted a faint snore. The beast at rest. No one thought of closing the door.

"What happened to Evan?" Gareth asked his mother, whispering even behind the closed kitchen door. "He's like another person."

"He's ill, dear," Mrs. Lloyd told him.

"Is it — the wound?" Siôn asked.

His mother nodded. "Doctors have pills for that sort of thing now," Siôn said helpfully, and then, worried by his mother's closed uncomfortable expression, "He'll get better, won't he, Mom?"

"Oh Siôn, I don't know," she confessed. "I hope so!"

At three o'clock the twins thankfully departed for a friend's Halloween party. Mrs. Lloyd took Bethan to visit Iolo. "He'd like to see you, too," she told Nia, offering her a way of escape. "He's much better now, not so gloomy."

"I'll stay," Nia said firmly.

Catrin gave the remaining family their tea before she left for the community center with her father. "It's only up the road, so if you need us . . ." she said meaningfully to Nia. "Or would you rather come with us?"

Nia shook her head. "Nerys will be here. We'll keep each other company," she said. They didn't mention the sleeping soldier. She followed Catrin and her father into the hall, where Mr. Lloyd switched on the light. None of them looked into the room where he lay, though Nia could have described his attitude exactly. One arm hung loose, its gold-and-bronze ornaments caught in a bright beam that slid through the open door.

Mr. Lloyd moved uneasily from one foot to the other. "Perhaps you'd better come with us, girl," he said.

"Then poor Nerys will be alone," Nia said, hoping to remind her father of the tear that had been wrung from his eldest child.

"Ah yes." As he and Catrin stepped out of the house, the streetlights came on. It was dusk. Nia closed the door. She went back to the kitchen and sat at the table. Above her, Nerys creaked across a room. The light seemed to be fading in seconds.

It has to be now, Nia told herself, *another day might be too late.* She forced herself into the hall again and stood on the brink of the dark room where he slept. Would he detect the lie in her voice? She took a deep breath and walked in.

"Evan," she called faintly into his sleep, then gaining courage, loud and steadily, "Evan! Evan!"

His eyes opened, and for a brief moment, her own dear prince looked out. The sorrowful blue gaze shook all her resolve. He knew. She couldn't trust herself to speak. But the dark soul betrayed him. Something stirred behind his eyes, leaking tiny yellow flames into the blue. Nia was tipped into action and the lies came pouring out. "Catrin wants you. She's on the bridge. She sent me to fetch you. It's urgent, she says." Shame confined her voice to a tight little croak, and she was sure he could see deep inside her where the truth lay all mixed up with love and dread.

But he swung his legs onto the floor, stood up, rubbed his eyes, and walked past her. In the hall he touched her shoulder with his ringed fingers and said quietly, "Thank you, Nia!" She longed to keep his hand and hold him back, but he whisked himself away and was gone.

She waited behind the closed door then suddenly flung it open and leaped out. The town was deserted except for the tall figure striding toward the bridge. Rehearsals were in full swing and the "Sanctus" came pouring into the street like water; it washed around the soldier, causing him to stop and lift his head in a listening attitude as though he was willing the music to keep him there, safe from the future. Slowly he released himself and continued on his way. The rain had stopped but the wet pavement glimmered gold under the streetlights.

Close to the houses, Nia followed, watching every movement of the man ahead. When he walked onto the bridge, she slid behind a wide buttress at the end and peeped out. Evan was alone, staring over the wall at the wild flood.

Where was Gwyn? Suppose he let her down? Would Evan, sensing the trick, rush furiously back to her? And then something that had been there all the time began to move. It was an indistinct form, topped with a cloud of white, startling in the twilight.

The soldier turned and faced the magician.

❄ ❄ ❄

All through the day Gwyn had been torn by indecision. Perhaps, after all, he wouldn't have to exert himself. He thought of using the telephone to postpone the meeting. The persistent rain and the distant, forlorn murmur of thunder made him restless. But toward dusk he became very calm. He went to fetch his ash wand and was amazed by the energy it sent through him.

When the rain had stopped and the melancholy sky waited for night, Gwyn began his journey to Pendewi. He had to wield the wand carefully, for when it struck the ground a hollow sound came from it, as though its echo reached to the world's beginning. Every chime filled him with a wonderful optimism, but he didn't want to alert the countryside. He discovered that Arianwen was traveling with him, crouched in a little hollow at the top of the stick. She had decided to play a part, it seemed, though Gwyn couldn't guess what it would be.

He passed Idris Llewelyn's chapel, and the unicorn, remade and even more beautiful, beckoned him on into the land where he would make the last spell of his childhood. Tomorrow he would be thirteen. He felt invincible.

Yet when he saw the soldier, peering into the deadly water, a little qualm kept him at the end of the bridge where a damp mist wrapped him safely out of sight, tempting him to retreat. But he could feel the wand aching like one of his own limbs, and he moved onto the bridge. They were quite alone now, he and the soldier, together on an island, from which only one of them would return.

All at once the soldier, feeling his presence, turned to face him, and Gwyn almost lost his courage, for another creature swooped out of Evan Llŷr, adding extra height to his already tall frame. A great warrior stood there, shining with royal jewels, and a scowl of such hatred coursed out of the familiar features, it took all Gwyn's strength to look at it. But he held steady, and without averting his eyes, brought the broken horse from his pocket and held it out.

His action was greeted by a dreadful sound, deeper than any natural voice. It rolled around his head, confusing all his senses and threatened, "You'll die this time, old man, if you attempt to keep me in that!"

His hatred towers above anything I can feel, Gwyn thought and began to weaken. But, once more, the ash wand jerked against his fingers, and an icy glow, perched on the tip, floated across and settled in the crest of bright hair. The warrior hardly noticed it. He took a step toward Gwyn. The wand bowed in the magician's hand, alive with energy. It twisted toward the wall, and a shaft of light traveled from it deep into the stones.

They burst into fragments and tumbled into the river, leaving a jagged hole that opened onto the still rising tide of water.

Again the warrior bellowed but this time Gwyn detected a note of anxiety, a loss of confidence. The spider had begun to work. Tiny threads crisscrossed the monster's face. He tried to brush them away but the spider floated out of reach and spun on faster and faster, over the plume of chestnut hair, across the eyes, forming a ghostly mask. The soldier took another step toward Gwyn; again he swept his hands over his face, this time clutching the air as though he would crush it with his huge fists. He leaned forward; powerful, shining arms reached toward Gwyn, who knew that if this warrior fell he meant to take the magician with him. Helplessly, Gwyn closed his eyes so that what followed became a secret ceremony, known only to the men from the past, leaving the two who remained forever doubtful of what had happened.

Gwyn only knew that his right hand became a weapon wielded by someone else. It raised the wand and struck something with such furious energy that he was rocked off his feet. He opened his eyes, wondering how he should protect himself from the assault that must follow. But the bridge was empty and beyond the breached wall, there was a man in the water, struggling for his life.

"I don't hate you," Gwyn called across the water. "Forgive me, Evan Llŷr."

An answer came from Evan Llŷr: a drowning howl that carried on the waves like receding music, an age-old lament composed of many voices. And then a girl tore past Gwyn crying, "Gwyn Griffiths, you have murdered my cousin!" And Nia bounded down the bank, following the current that bore Evan Llŷr away.

Nia, racing beside the river, couldn't understand why the town was still singing. Her prince was drowning. All the hosannas in the world couldn't save him now. She tore helplessly along the bank, trying to keep pace with the current, calling "Evan" endlessly, as though the name could keep him safe. Three times she saw his arm strike through the gray tide, the last time was hardly a stroke at all, but more a lonely gesture of farewell.

She sank onto the wet grass and turned her face away from the river where all her happy dreams had died. But a surprising gust of wind urged her to look again. On the far side of the river where slim alders clustered on the bank, the wind, in a sudden frenzy, tore at the red leaves, dispatching them in a cloud across the torrent. Startled birds flew out, calling to one another in alarm. It seemed to Nia that every bird she had ever known had a place in the great flock that soared above her, their wingbeats clattering into the air like a mighty orchestra.

Then into the band of golden sky that rimmed the distant hill, a line of horsemen drew up and began to descend toward the wooded bank. Nia's vision was blurred by tears, and they seemed to seep through the naked trees like drifting streams of smoke, but she could still make out the dull bronze of spears and helmets and the occasional glitter of gold.

Struggling against unreality, Nia watched the silent, shadowy army follow their prince beneath the water, safe into the

Otherworld. She watched until every tiny gleam had drowned, until the bank was deserted and the river, the same unassailable sweep of water as before. Then she made her way back to the bridge.

She found a crowd of men surrounding Gwyn Griffiths, who lay perilously close to the place where Evan had slipped into the river. He looked bewildered and years younger than the last time she had seen him. There was an old stick beside him that looked as if it had been struck by lightning, and his hands, clasped around something small and black, were bleeding. Making her way across his sleeve was a tiny silver spider.

"Doesn't seem to know where he is," someone remarked. Nia recognized Morgan the Smithy.

"Come on, lad," another said. "You'd better move from there. It's dangerous!"

"A man fell in," Gwyn said dreamily. "I couldn't save him."

"In that?" asked Morgan in disbelief, nodding at the angry current.

"It was my cousin, Evan Llŷr," Nia murmured through unspent tears.

"Then he's gone, girl, that's for sure," said Morgan. "That flood would take the strongest man alive!"

CHAPTER TWELVE
The Hopeful Prince

HE HAD NO RIGHT TO BE OUTSIDE HER ROOM, TAPPING AWAY like an intrusive woodpecker. The door was open anyway, and Gwyn could see that she didn't want company. Why didn't he go away?

"Nia, you've got to talk to me!" He came in cautiously, hands in pockets, while she quickly hid her treasure on the bed beside her. "What's that you've got?" He looked so jaunty.

"Nothing," she replied sullenly.

He came and sat beside her.

The whole world ached. A grim mist had lain in the valley for days, a ghostly shroud left to shame them. A heavy, feature-less climate hung around the town, only the mountain rose above it. Impossible events had set Pendewi adrift from the universe, untouched and unloved. No one wanted to know about a soldier who had carried a family into his dark past. Some things were better left unsaid, it seemed. For weeks Nia hadn't even heard his name.

"Nia, he's not dead!"

When she had taken in the full meaning of what he said, she stared at him stupidly, her life upside down again.

"He swam ashore downriver," Gwyn told her gently. "Didn't know his name for a while. He's been in the hospital."

"Why didn't Mom tell me?"

"They've only just heard. And you two girls have been so frantic, we thought it would be better to break it gradually."

"Is he coming back?"

"How could he, Nia?" His dark eyes, truthful and very kind, held hers.

She turned away.

"I cured him, Nia," he said firmly.

"You tried to murder him!"

"No, not Evan. It was that other one. I was trying to save Evan. I had a head full of spells, and Arianwen ready to convert him, but my ancestor had a mind of his own. Perhaps he doubted my will, so he reached through me to quiet Efnisien forever, not caring how he did it. He didn't know our soldier, you see!"

She felt behind her and brought the little carving onto her lap. "I found this in the reeds beside the river," she said. "It's yours, isn't it?"

The paint had washed off and the soldier looked like little more than a piece of wood, the face and clothing vaguely sketched in lines of fine silt.

"It was a mistake," he confessed. "I thought of those little sacrificial figures they found in Celtic springs, thrown there to heal the owners of some dreadful illness. I don't know what I expected. I certainly didn't realize that he'd fight it and bring a storm to your home."

"Well, you'll never save him now," Nia said dramatically.

"He *is* saved," Gwyn told her cheerfully.

She looked up. "What do you mean?"

"Gwydion may have done his worst, but his descendant won a battle, too!" He brought from his pocket a wooden horse that resembled the animal she'd found in Evan's room. If it was the same horse, it was transformed. Polished and handsome, its severed features all restored, it glowed.

"Is it . . . ?" she began.

"The same," Gwyn confirmed.

"What happened? It's so beautiful."

"This is how it was in the beginning, when Gwydion's brother gave it as a gift, before it was used for magic. Gwydion told me." She darted him a suspicious look that he refused to acknowledge, plowing on in spite of her impatient fidgeting. "After he'd — gone into the water, the horse began to kick in my hands and when I wouldn't let go, it punished me. I don't know how I held on, but it was something I had to do, to cling on and soak up all the anger. It seemed to reach every part of me with hooves and teeth and bony head. I hung on until the pain knocked me out, and when I came to my hands were bleeding, but the horse was— like this!"

"What does it mean?" she asked, wanting only to hear about her prince.

"Efnisien's anger is all spent. He's a hopeful prince now, riding through the Otherworld."

"But Evan?"

Gwyn shrugged. "It's hard to say. Perhaps we'll know one day if he's forgiven us."

He saved his prince, Nia thought, *but left mine wandering without a soul, alone and unforgiving.* "Can I keep this?" she held up the wooden effigy.

"As a substitute? If you like." He got up and walked away from her. He seemed like such a sunny person now, she hardly knew him. But when he reached the door, he turned back and said almost bashfully, "By the way, there's something else."

"More good news!" she said, more resentfully than she'd intended.

"In a way," he said, still cheerful. "Look!"

She looked at him and saw nothing but Gwyn Griffiths, black hair rather too long and bushy, not even halfway to being well-built, a lean face with eyes so dark they could conceal a thousand mysteries, and an annoyingly smiley mouth.

"My ankles!" he said, directing her gaze to a pair of wrinkled gray socks.

"I can see your ankles. They're fantastic!"

"Don't be like that, Nia!"

"Your pants have shrunk!"

He beamed at her. She seemed to have found the right answer. "Not at all. My pants have not shrunk. I've grown. Two inches to be precise."

He looked, all at once, so shy and so joyful she couldn't deny him his congratulations. "Well done," she said, and before she could bite it back, "You'll be a giant!"

"Hardly," he returned. "Average will do for me!"

Average he will never be, she thought and, with one of her queer little spins into the future, saw an unusually fine young man, glowing with secret knowledge and as mysteriously handsome as a mature magician should be.

❋ ❋ ❋

Nia took her wooden soldier to school every day after that. She wrapped him in a piece of velvet and kept him at the bottom of her backpack. At night she would tuck him under her pillow. Once he fell out of the backpack, and Dewi Davis pounced on the little figure, threw him in the air, and launched him into a game of catch. Nia, helpless with inexplicable rage, wept for its return, but this only drove Dewi's gang to heap further indignities on the soldier. They kicked it across the playground, purposely tripping and treading on it. It wasn't restored to her until Gwyn came out and thumped Dewi on the chin. The game stopped abruptly. Dewi was afraid of Gwyn.

"Why don't you keep it at home?" Gwyn said, putting the soldier safe into her hands.

"I can't," she replied. "He'd be alone."

Gwyn shook his head. "You've got to snap out of it, Nia!"

She couldn't. Someone had to keep the faith.

Catrin was almost her old self again. The enchanted kiss was fading and she began to blossom with extraordinary talent. The piano rocked under a passionate torrent of sonatas, preludes, and fugues. She'd passed her exams with distinction. A few days after her exam results had arrived, Michael McGoohan came by with a congratulatory bouquet. Catrin received her visitor warily. They spent half an hour in the living room, then Michael went home. The following week he took her to a concert. Michael had embarked on a second diffident courtship. Catrin had emerged from her association with Evan mysteriously glamourized. She was definitely not going to be an easy conquest, but obviously well worth the effort.

"What if Evan comes back?" Nia asked her sister one day.

"What if?" Catrin airily replied. She was cured of the kiss. That part of the book would remain closed, never to be reopened. It was just an episode on Catrin's route to being seventeen. If she was aware that she'd been a heroine in someone else's story, the knowledge belonged only to her.

When Iolo returned home, his bones healed quickly but it took him a long time to become a cheerful little boy again. Gradually, with Nia's help, he spent less and less of his time remembering the shining spirit who had tricked him. One day he even ventured, "Nia, will we see Evan again?"

To which she replied, "Perhaps, if we all want him enough."

"I do!" Iolo said.

If he hadn't been too old for sisterly embraces, she would have hugged him.

❋ ❋ ❋

At Christmas they had a short letter from Evan Llŷr, tucked inside a card. It was like a letter from a stranger. He thanked them for their hospitality and was sorry for any trouble he had caused. There was no return address.

Nia begged to keep the card, not string it up with all the

others on a silver ribbon. No one objected. She took it to her room and tried to read some special message in the picture. But there was nothing there. Only a decorative golden "Greetings" on an emerald background. *At least it isn't red,* she thought. And took comfort from that.

She decided to color her soldier for the festivities. She went to Idris Llewelyn's studio for advice and found Emlyn working there. "Do you want me to paint him the way he was before?" he asked. "Or give him a different character? I could carve the helmet away and give him a good head of hair."

Nia thought about it, and remembering the way Evan had looked on that very first, long-ago day, described him to Emlyn.

"I'll bring it around tomorrow," he said.

That wouldn't do. She couldn't be without her soldier, she explained. Intrigued but obliging, Emlyn let her wait in the chapel until he had finished the work and then walked home with her. The paint was still wet and she held it before her on outstretched palms, like a precious offering.

Outside her front door Emlyn suddenly asked, "What are you up to, Nia? There's nothing very special about that carving. It's only chestnut wood and paint!"

"I have to keep him safe," she told Emlyn. "No one else will."

"You ought to get out more," he said. "I'm going to the movies next week. *Apeman's Revenge* is on. Do you want to come?"

It wasn't her sort of film, but surprising herself, she said, "Yes."

As it was they went in a foursome: she and Emlyn, Alun and

Gwyn. But she was aware of a subtle difference in their relationships. She'd achieved a new position in the group and hadn't tagged along as just one of the boys.

She kept her carving wrapped up in wool all through the long winter and the chilly spring. She even made a scarf for him and a felt hat with a golden band. Now he was a little prince.

Nerys came upon the bundle, tucked in a towel beside Nia's place on the kitchen bench. "You're too old for this, Nia," Nerys complained. "Why don't you give it to Bethan?"

"He's mine," Nia cried vehemently, snatching her toy from Nerys. "Leave him alone."

"Willingly," said Nerys. "Just keep him out of my way!" She knew who it was meant to be. Emlyn had done his work well. Nerys still hadn't forgiven Evan for that tear.

One May weekend, Mr. and Mrs. Lloyd took a vacation. They went to the sea and left their children with their friends. Catrin and Nerys stayed at home, the boys went to the Griffithses' farm, Nia and Bethan to Tŷ Llŷr.

Nia was blissful in her old home. The Llewelyns had made it so alive and beautiful. On her first evening she took her toy prince up the lane to visit Nain Griffiths.

"He's very fine," Nain said, regarding the little figure that stood on the summit of her tallest pile of books. Nia had supplied him with a new fur cape and a gold belt made of Christmas string.

"He's out there, somewhere, all alone," Nia said, knowing she would be understood. "He went away believing that we'd rather he didn't exist. But we were his family, the only people in the whole world he could trust. I wish I could tell him that I'm sorry."

"Perhaps he knows." Nain took the little figure from its perch and stroked the soft fur cape.

"Then why doesn't he tell us where he is or if he's well?" Nia burst out. "It's not fair. Gwyn has saved his old prince. He's got all that magic piled inside him and ancestors to back him up but he can't seem to help my cousin."

"You're doing that," Nain said gently. "If you care as much for him as you do this little carving, then he'll know."

"How?" Nia asked, frowning.

"One has ways." She smiled enigmatically. "Remember what I said about Ares and Aphrodite?"

"I'm not a love goddess," Nia said sheepishly.

Nain laughed and put the toy prince into her hands. "You don't have to be a goddess!"

It was getting dark when Nia began to walk back to Tŷ Llŷr. The candle blossoms on the chestnut tree glowed white against the evening sky. Nia stopped and gazed at the tree, imagining the blossoms to be real white flames. When she half closed her eyes she thought she could make out a familiar face smiling down at her. It was so lightly etched into the shadow it could have been a wisp of lichen clinging to a branch, yet gradually she became sure of what she was seeing and knew at last with joyful certainty that it was the true forgiving prince and that every candle was a lost soldier, peacefully remembered.

She laid her wooden prince beneath the tree, covered him with last year's leaves, and went back to Tŷ Llŷr.

It was Nain Griffiths's birthday in June. She wanted a special celebration, she said, for herself and Gwyn, whose thirteenth birthday had been overshadowed by Evan's disappearance. The whole family must be there: Llewelyns, Griffiths, and even the Lloyds, who were part of her family even if not directly related. They would have a party in the field behind her house. The weather would be glorious.

Gwyn sensed buried excitement in his grandmother. She was keeping the lid on a delicious secret, something that she would save until the very last moment, to flabbergast them all when they least expected it.

"I'll pay you back if you spring something nasty on us," he warned.

"Wizard!" she snapped. "Whatever gave you that idea?" She had made a primrose-yellow dress for herself (the color of insanity, Gwyn had told her) and was flaunting it a week too soon, for his approval. "You never had your party because of all that — trouble. So we'll have a double celebration and I'll make a towering cake. By the way," she lowered her voice, "will the ancestor be with us?"

Gwyn laughed. "He's been gone for ages, Nain. The mirror tells me I'm thirteen and just the right size. It seems a long, long time since you brought me those five gifts. They've taken me on a strange journey but now I feel I've finished with them. I'm grateful for the adventure but I don't believe I'll need magic for a while. Arianwen will keep me company, but as a peaceful friend. I won't use seaweed and a scarf to bring my sister back to me; I'll let her stay in the place where she's happiest. And the horse, as I've shown you, is a precious ornament. I'll never need to hide him now."

"That was your greatest achievement, Gwyn," Nain said thoughtfully, "to bring the dark prince peace at last. No one else could do it!" And then, all at once remembering the strange toy her great-great-grandmother, the witch, had left in her keeping, she asked, "But what has become of the pipe?"

"Ah, I exchanged the pipe," Gwyn said, "for an ash stick — a wand to keep me in touch with all my ghostly relatives."

"Perhaps it comes from a tree that fathered my own woods," Nain suggested happily, more to herself than Gwyn.

"It feeds me, Nain," Gwyn told. "It gives me so much energy I feel I'll reach the clouds someday."

"I wish you could spare some for your little friend," Nain said.

"Nia? Yes, she does look a bit weary."

"I never knew a child could store up so much loyalty," his grandmother said thoughtfully. "She'll be rewarded though."

"Nain, what have you planned?" He had an inkling of what it might be, but still couldn't really guess it.

"Nothing! Nothing! Now go home and leave me to plot!"

✳ ✳ ✳

It was a glorious day. Three families in a field of flowers, mown just enough to spread a huge white cloth, covered in treats. In the center, a gaudy five-layered birthday cake listed crazily in the breeze, the leaning tower of Pisa surrounded by Nain's cookies, fruitcake, and endless plates of sandwiches. And not to be outdone, Gwyn's mother had contributed two versions of her prizewinning sponge cake, one chocolate and one vanilla.

"How old are you, Nain Griffiths?" Nia asked. "There are only thirteen candles on the cake!"

"The candles are for Gwyn," she said. "*I* am ageless, and anyway, I've forgotten."

When all the plates were empty she still wouldn't cut the cake. "Play a game," she commanded. "You're still not ready for my treat!"

Nia had a feeling she wasn't referring to the cake. She joined in an unruly game of baseball. Out of danger, on the far side of the field, Catrin and Michael lay in a pool of buttercups, feeding each other with whispers. Neither of them was aware that, from a distance, Idris Llewelyn was capturing their mood with colored pencils.

Nia watched Nain Griffiths tiptoe lightly over to the artist, all brimming with excitement, as though she longed to share some wonderful secret. *Maybe she has made magic somewhere,* Nia thought. *Maybe there's a genie in the woods, waiting to grant us all three wishes. I could make do with just one.*

Something sailed over her head and bounced into the lane beyone the hedge. "Neeeeaaa!" came seven shouts. She ran and flung herself over the gate. Gwyn, not trusting her speed, was hard on her heels. But Nain came to open the gate and called him back.

The ball trickled down the lane, teasing her with unpredictable little twists and turns. At last it came to rest, wedged safely on the stony roadside. But she didn't pick it up. A stranger was approaching: a tall figure with raven hair and something thrown around his shoulders in the manner of a cloak. Not strange at all when she came to study him.

The mountain lurched, the trees spun, and the earth rolled away from her feet. She could feel the welcome that Nain and Gwyn were restraining so that it should belong only to her. It was as though they had jumped off a seesaw and left her tumbling in a dangerously fast descent. It might have ended in disaster if he hadn't caught her.

"Evan Llŷr has come to trouble you again," he said, holding her very tight.

She knew it wasn't true. He was her prince, but in a way, quite new, his gaze untroubled and his smile completely hopeful.

About Jenny Nimmo

I was born in Windsor, Berkshire, England, and educated at boarding schools in Kent and Surrey from the age of six until I was sixteen, when I ran away from school to become a drama student/assistant stage manager with Theater South East. I graduated and acted in repertory theater in various towns and cities.

I left Britain to teach English to three Italian boys in Amalfi, Italy. On my return, I joined the BBC, first as a picture researcher, then assistant floor manager, studio manager (news), and finally director/adaptor with *Jackanory* (a BBC storytelling program for children). I left the BBC to marry Welsh artist David Wynn-Millward and went to live in Wales in my husband's family home. We live in a very old converted water mill, and the river is constantly threatening to break in, which it has done several times in the past, most dramatically on my youngest child's first birthday. During the summer, we run a residential school of art, and I have to move my office, put down tools (typewriter and pencils), and don an apron and cook! We have three grown-up children, Myfanwy, Ianto, and Gwenhwyfar.